W9-BBQ-318

3 1230 00588

H-05

The Dreams

The Dreams

Naguib Mahfouz

Translated by Raymond Stock

The American University in Cairo Press
Cairo ✺ New York

The American University in Cairo Press
113 Sharia Kasr el Aini, Cairo, Egypt
420 Fifth Avenue, New York, NY 10018
www.aucpress.com

Dar el Kutub No. 7955/04
ISBN 977 424 866 X

Designed by Andrea El-Akshar/AUC Press Design Center
Printed in Egypt

Translator's Introduction

Could we but give us wholly to the dreams,
And get into their world that to the sense
Is shadow, and not linger wretchedly
Among insubstantial things . . .
                        —William Butler Yeats [1]

On Friday, October 14, 1994, an Islamist militant, allegedly acting on orders from blind Egyptian cleric Omar Abd al-Rahman, stabbed Naguib Mahfouz twice in the neck with a switchblade as he sat in a car outside his Nileside home in Greater Cairo. The young man who attacked the then 82-year-old author, the first Arab to be awarded the Nobel Prize in literature, clearly intended to silence him forever. Though the assault, which damaged the nerve that controls his right arm and hand, did prevent him from writing for over four years, the fanatic's mission failed. [2] Not only did Mahfouz survive this nightmarish crime—he lived to tell us his dreams.

Yet the path to the present highly innovative and provocative work was not an easy one, and near its end came a brief, but very revealing, musical interlude. On February 14, 1999, after prolonged and intensive physiotherapy, Mahfouz began to unveil his first new writing since the attempt on his life, with a brief work called *al-Aghani* ("The Songs"), in a Cairo women's magazine, *Nisf al-dunya*

("Half the World"), where he had been publishing all his latest fiction since the periodical first appeared in 1990. (After the attempt on his life, the same magazine continued to feature stories he had written prior to that tragedy until *al-Aghani* debuted.) More a tribute to memory than to imagination, *al-Aghani* is a series of deftly-chosen quotations from popular Egyptian tunes, ranging back through more than nine decades, that capture the spirit and mood of the various stages of Mahfouz's life, from childhood to old age. The first work he has published in colloquial Egyptian, it is also so far the only one made up entirely of verse.

A few months later, a new stream of Mahfouz stories once again began to appear in the pages of *Nisf al-dunya*. This was a succession of numbered, extremely brief narratives, which one could easily term 'nanonovellas,' bearing the title *Ahlam fatrat al-naqaha*—literally, "Dreams of the Period of Recovery." They were almost completely unlike anything Mahfouz—or anyone else, for that matter—had published before. Yet the "almost" here is crucial, especially as far as this author's own past work is concerned.

In a 1982 collection of Mahfouz's short fiction called *Ra'aytu fima yara al-na'im* ("I Saw as the Sleeper Sees"), the title piece is a series of 17 short, numbered 'dreams'—each no more than a few paragraphs in length.[3] Meant to read like accounts of actual dreams, each begins with the phrase that gave the work its name. In a study of these 'dreams,' Arabic literary scholar Fedwa Malti-Douglas notes that many are drawn from Mahfouz's reading of both the medieval adventure-poems (*maqamat*) of Badi' al-Zaman al-Hamadhani and the modern allegorical ghost story by Muhammad al-Muwaylihi derived from them, *Hadith 'Isa ibn Hisham* ("The Tale of 'Isa ibn Hisham," 1898 in newspaper serial,

1907 as a book). In the seventeenth and final one of these cryptic, highly imaginative stories by Mahfouz, the dreamer—while watching a nickelodeon on humanity's progress through ancient civilizations to the exploration of space—feels a delirious desire to fly to the moon. Yet weighted down with medals and other honors, he is at first unable to move from his seat. Finally he manages to shed these encumbrances—which perhaps ironically presage the medallion and diploma of Mahfouz's 1988 Nobel—and levitate as desired to his lunar liberation from the bonds of earth. Or—as Malti-Douglas shrewdly projects it forward—from the enchaining enthusiasm of his teeming admirers after he won the most renowned award in his field, the Nobel.

Malti-Douglas also points out that *Ra'aytu fima yara al-na'im* deliberately harks back to the ancient (and continuing) Arabic tradition of presenting (and interpreting) dreams. Even the title itself, she observes, is a variation on the sentence that typically begins a dream narrative in this genre: *Ra'aytu fi-al-manam* ("I saw in a dream").[4] The extraordinary interest that dreams have long aroused among the Arabs can be found, for example, in the often oneiristic chronicles of Abu Ali ibn al-Banna, who lived in eleventh-century Baghdad. Frequently dreams bring back the dead, who (as in Mahfouz's Dream 89 of this volume) scold the living. Al-Banna recounts that

> Abu'l-'Abbas b. ash-Shatti was accompanying me. He related to me two old dreams about Ibn al-Tustariya al-Hanbali—may God have mercy upon him! He said, 'I saw him in my dream, and I greeted him. He returned my greeting, and took hold of a kerchief which was on my

head, with both hands, tied it, and said, "O Abu-'l-'Abbas! What is this rudeness which I have not experienced before?'" My informant continued, 'I had stopped visiting his tomb; so I resumed my visits and continued doing so without interruption."⁵

Or (with ironic reference to current events), dreams could invoke the fear of foreign invasion, which, at least potentially, can be an omen of ultimate good fortune:

> In another dream, it appeared as though there were a great swarm of green locusts, each of them holding a pearl in his mouth. They represent armies coming; and it is possible that their coming might be beneficial. For green represents worldly prosperity, and pearls represent the Qur'an and religion. Hence, it is possible that there need be no fear as regards their coming—if God so wills!⁶

Today's politics naturally intrude in Mahfouz's current dreams. Most dramatic, perhaps, are the apparent allusions to his views of the Arab–Israeli conflict (Dream 90) and the war on terrorism (Dreams 74 and 103). But these are in the eyes of the reader, of course—and he has always encouraged others to reach their own conclusions about what he is saying.

Recently I asked Mahfouz what he thought was the greatest difference between *Ra'aytu fima yara al-na'im* and *The Dreams*. Without hesitation, he replied, "Composition." The earlier work, he explained, was entirely a conscious authorial creation, while each episode of the present project is "a[n actual] dream, which I develop into a story."[7] In this, he may have achieved the major ambition of the iconoclast André Breton, who declared in the *Surrealist Manifesto* (1924), "I believe in the future resolution of these two states—outwardly so contradictory—which are dream and reality, into a sort of absolute reality, a surreality, so to speak."[8]

Mahfouz began his novelistic career with a series of three books set in the pharaonic era: *Khufu's Wisdom* (1939), *Rhadopis of Nubia* (1943), and *Thebes at War* (1944), which indirectly critique contemporary society in symbolic terms.[9] But he is best known for his 'realistic' works such as *Midaq Alley* (1947), *The Beginning and the End* (1949), *The Cairo Trilogy* (*Palace Walk, Palace of Desire,* and *Sugar Street* (1956–57), and more. Yet Mahfouz has also been experimenting with virtually every style and type of fiction since serializing the book that later nearly got him killed—*Children of the Alley,* itself a highy symbolic allegory of mankind's corrupt ascent from the days of Adam and Eve to the era of modern science, set in a mythologized Gamaliya. As it ran in daily installments in Cairo's flagships newspaper, *al-Ahram,* in the fall of 1959, a group of shaykhs from al-Azhar—Egypt's great center of Islamic orthodoxy—denounced it for purportedly besmirching God and the prophets by representing them as earthly characters with human flaws. Demonstrations erupted at local mosques, and the government of President Gamal Abd al-Nasser banned the novel's appearance as a book in Egypt—though permitting its publication abroad. With respect to Arabic publication, the ban still holds—at least so far as al-Azhar is concerned—and Mahfouz's failure to 'repent' for it led to his near-murder in 1994. (Intriguingly, both these works—*Children of the Alley* and *The Dreams*—mark new beginnings in the use of allegory, and each is connected to the attempt on his life: one as an indirect cause, the other as an indirect result thereof.)

By the late 1960s, Mahfouz turned to ever more radical forms, including absurdist plays of pure dialogue, and stories that have grown shorter and increasingly compact over time. And so the often prevailing view among literary critics in his country that Mahfouz is a plodding nineteenth-century novelist compared to those of younger generations—none of whom have yet matched his magisterial output in either quality or quantity—would seem to be the most wistful of envious dreams.

In the case of *The Dreams*, the effort to produce at all has been especially difficult for Mahfouz. Apart from the damage done by the assailant's knife, he has endured diabetes since the early 1960s. Though controlled through a rigid diet (typical of his ironbound personal discipline), over time, the disease and the years themselves have enormously weakened his eyesight and hearing. Long before this tragic incident, he could write only "by the feel of the shape of the letters," as he told me once in the early 1990s. Then, he was twice hospitalized (once for pneumonia, the second time for a cardio-vascular crisis) in the winter of 2003. During his first stay in hospital, he confided to Mohamed Salmawy, who interviews him every week for his regularly weekly column in *al-Ahram*, *Hiwarat Najib Mahfuz* ("Dialogues with Naguib Mahfouz,") that he no longer dreamt when he slept—though he could continue to publish the material he had already stored for some time to come. "My drawer is still full," he reassured Salmawy.[10]

Adding to his travails that season, during a fall in his apartment he evidently broke a small bone in his right wrist. From that point on, if not before, Mahfouz began to dictate his new writing—

something he had previously refused even to consider. Luckily, however, he soon had new dreams to relate. Though he complains of little sleep, the time he does have to dream seems to be fertile. The result has been some of his most remarkable writing ever. Indeed, *The Dreams* are a unique and haunting mixture of the deceptively quotidian, the seductively lyrical, and the savagely nightmarish—the richly condensed sum of more than four-score-and-ten years of artistic genius and everyday experience. He has even lamented to reporter Youssef Rakha of *al-Ahram* that "Now writing is restricted to the dreams." He added ruefully, "It seems I gave myself the evil eye when I wrote *Ra'aytu fima yara al-na'im* [*I Saw as the Sleeper Sees*]."[11]

As in anyone's nighttime visions, real memory and experience permeate *The Dreams*. Close friends long deceased often appear, as in the case of Dr. Husayn Fawzi (1900–88) in Dream 86, former permanent undersecretary to the Minister of Culture, an ophthalmologist famed for his study and patronage of western classical music, and for his travel writing[12]—the latter gaining him the sobriquet, "the Egyptian Sinbad." And there are teachers from his youth, such as Shaykh Muharram (Dream 6), one of the young Mahfouz's two Arabic instructors in his secondary school in then-suburban Abbasiya, and his math teacher in the same period, Hamza Effendi (Dream 27). *The Dreams* recall them less kindly than Fawzi. Some other figures from real life, who receive similarly sarcastic handling, are identified only by their initials, as in Dreams 72 and 73.

Inevitably, there are also references to Mahfouz's past writings. In Dream 10, the "pharaonic queen" is Nitocris, the widow (and sister) of King Merenra II—characters in Mahfouz's second published novel, *Rhadopis of Nubia*. The revenge she takes on her husband's murderers is from a legend recorded by the ancient Greek writers Herodotus and Strabo. In a freakishly intertextual incident, the woman who endowed the first major literary prize that Mahfouz would win (for *Rhadopis of Nubia*, in 1940)—Qut al-Qulub al-Damardashiya—is evidently the dangerous lady with a dainty gun in Dream 81.

And Mahfouz has been a writer not only for the printed page. In Dream 13, his unconscious self meets a girl who identifies herself as "Rayya's daughter." To his horror, she then adds, "Maybe you remember Rayya and Sakina." Very few Egyptians who lived through the time of their vicious career, or who have seen the 1953 film about them—written by Naguib Mahfouz (who created many of the most praised scenarios in the history of Arab cinema) and directed by the legendary Salah Abu Seif—could ever forget them. Rayya and Sakina were women in the forties who lured gullible young members of their sex to their homes in Alexandria, where they were chloroformed and killed for their jewelry by a gang led by the malignant pair's husbands. Before their apprehension in 1921, they had claimed up to thirty victims, whom they buried in the houses in which they had died.[13]

Equally inevitable is an apparition of Mahfouz's greatest personal hero, Sa'd Pasha Zaghlul (1859?–1927), leader of the 1919 movement for Egyptian independence from Britain (Dream 73).[14] And in Dreams 30 and 48, Mahfouz mentions the mightiest musician that movement produced, the Alexandrian minstrel–composer Sayyid Darwish (1892–1923).[15] A line from one of Darwish's most famous songs, which Mahfouz chose to end his novel *Palace Walk*, the first in the *Trilogy*, could well represent one of the central themes of *The Dreams* as well: "Visit me once each year, for it's wrong to abandon people forever."[16]

More than anything, however, *The Dreams* are a monument to the women that Mahfouz loved early in life, and whose images have never left him. Though happily married since 1954,[17] two of these now-distant bewitchments particularly possess him here, as in many other of his works. One is the "enchantress of Crimson Lane" (in Arabic, Darb Qirmiz, the narrow street in front of his first boyhood home in the old Islamic quarter of Gamaliya), in Dream 83. She has many incarnations throughout Mahfouz's vast *oeuvre,* as in his 1987 story, "Umm Ahmad" ("Mother of Ahmad"):

Crimson Lane has high stone walls; its doors are locked upon its secrets; there is no revealing of its mysteries without seeing them from within. There one sees a quarter for the poor folk and beggars gathered in the spot for their housework and to take care of their daily needs; and one sees a paradise singing with gardens, with a hall to receive visitors, and a harem for the ladies. And from the little high window just before the vaulted passage connecting the lane to its continuation beyond, sometimes appears a face luminous like the moon; I see it from the window of my little house that looks out over the lane and I wander, despite my infancy, in the magic of its beauty. I hear its melodious voice while it banters greetings with my mother when she passes out of the alley, and perhaps this is what impressed in my soul the love of song; Fatima al-'Umari, the unknown dream of childhood. . . .[18]

Just as unforgettable—to the reader as well as to Mahfouz himself—is the creature who stays ethereally out of reach to the writer, not only in Dreams 14, 84, and 85 but also elsewhere, particularly in his most celebrated work, the *Cairo Trilogy*. In the second volume, *Palace of Desire*, Mahfouz's admittedly autobiographical character, Kamal Ahmad Abd al-Jawad, is fatefully smitten (and ultimately rejected) by an aristocratic neighbor in Abbasiya—the same district to which Mahfouz's family moved from Gamaliya when he was about age ten. Mahfouz has said that the trauma of the actual lost teen romance upon which this was based afflicted him severely for about ten years—and remains vivid within him, more than seventy years later. (That his feelings were apparently never reciprocated—as in the *Trilogy*—could mean that Mahfouz has, in reality, been dreaming about a dream.[19])

In Dream 104, the last one in the current volume, it seems that the dreamer invites this person's apparition to a meeting with a mutual friend, now long dead, in a place where all were happy in days of yore. Her name, "the Lady Eye" as translated, is actually the spelling of the guttural Arabic letter *'ayn*, also meaning 'eye,' and at the same time the first letter of the name of Kamal's impossible love object in the *Trilogy*, Aida Shaddad. The man she is brought to meet is identified only as *al-mi'allim*, a dialect word meaning anything from shop owner, to top thug in a neighborhood, to head of a small business. One person it could have most suited in the Fishawi Café in the midst of Cairo's Khan al-Khalili bazaar, where the dream ends, is a man who used to sell Mahfouz books—who also happened to be sightless. Perhaps the blindness of love is at work here—and yet the woman whose very name signifies vision is the one scolded for failing to see.

Finally, *The Dreams* as a whole express the longings—and embody the bittersweet recollections—that Naguib Mahfouz enlists in *al-Aghani*, his heartbreakingly adept exercise in preserving the best of nearly a century of fleeting years and emotions through remembrance of the lyrics that capture them. The seventh and final section, "Old Age," is the most powerful of all. There can be no better way to close the introduction to a book of prose that in so many ways is truly poetry, than to present these verses for the first time in English:[20]

> When the evening comes . . .
> How long ago were we here?
> Old closeness from the beautiful past, if only
>   you could return.
> She said, how Time has mocked you since
>   our parting!
> And I told her, I seek refuge in God, but it
>   was you, not Time.
> What's gone is gone, O my heart . . .
> Say goodbye to your passion—forget it, and
>   forget me.
> Time that has gone will not come back again . . .
> I cannot forget you.
> We lived a lot and we saw a lot—
> And he who lives sees wonders.

As translator, I wish to thank Roger Allen, Walter Armbrust, Hazem Azmy, Brooke Comer, Shirley Johnston, Fuad Ahmed Noaman, Tawfik Saleh, and Husayn Ukasha for their generous help with the current work, as well as Jacinthe Assaad, Neil Hewison, Nadia Naqib, and Kelly Zaug for their deft and skillful editing. Most of all, I am grateful to Naguib Mahfouz, once more for his great openness and forbearance with my multifarious inquiries.

This translation is dedicated to my unwaveringly steadfast parents, John and Helen Stock—without whom it, or any other dreams of my own, would not have been possible.

Notes:

1 *Collected Poems of W. B. Yeats* (New York: MacMillan, 1956), p. 411. These lines are from a speech by Forgael in Yeats' verse play, *The Shadowy Waters* (1906), and are reproduced by permission of A.P. Watt on behalf of Michael B. Yeats.

2 After a swift and controversial military proceeding, two men were hanged and eleven others sent to prison for the attempt on Naguib Mahfouz's life and for plotting against the State. See Raymond Stock, "How Islamist Militants Put Egypt on Trial" (London: *The Financial Times,* Weekend FT, March 4/5, 1995), p. III.

3 See Naguib Mahfouz, *Ra'aytu fima yara al-na'im* (Cairo: Maktabat Misr, 1982), pp. 119–52.

4 Fedwa Malti-Douglas, "Mahfouz's Dreams" in *Naguib Mahfouz: From Regional Fame to Global Recognition*, ed. Michael Beard and Adnan Haydar, Syracuse University Press, 1993, pp. 126–43. For more on the *maqamat* of Badi' al-Zaman al-Hamadhani and *Hadith 'Isa ibn Hisham* by Muhammad al-Muwaylihi, see Roger Allen, *The Arabic Literary Heritage* (Cambridge: Cambridge University Press, 1988), p. 73.

5 George Makdisi, *History and Politics in 11th Century Baghdad* (Aldershot, Hamps. and Broofield, VT: Variorum, 1990), pp. 35–36.

6 *Ibid.,*pp. II/249–50.

7 Interview with Naguib Mahfouz, June 23, 2004.

8 As quoted by Ian Littlewood in *The Rough Guide Chronicle: France* (London: Rough Guides Ltd., 2002), p. 296. For an expansion on this theme, see Sarane Alexandrian, *Le Surréalisme et le rêve* (Paris: Gallimard, 1974).

9 *Khufu's Wisdom* (translated by Raymond Stock), *Rhadopis of Nubia* (translated by Anthony Calderbank) and *Kifah Tiba* (translated by Humphrey Davies) were all published by the American University in Cairo Press in 2003.

10 Mohamed Salmawy, "Wijhat Nazar: Hiwarat Najib Mahfuz," *al-Ahram*, Cairo, January 23, 2003, p. 12. Mahfouz had expressed similar frustration in an earlier period, when he felt unable to remember his dreams to record them, to Salmawy in "Wijhat Nazar," *al-Ahram,* September 12, 2002, p. 12.

11 Youssef Rakha, "Dreaming On," *Al-Ahram Weekly*, Cairo, December 11–17, 2003, p. 16. Mahfouz told Rakha that he had written Dreams 1–97 with his own hand before turning to dictation.

12 For a brief account of this prodigious figure's life, see Arthur Goldschmidt, *A Biographical Dictionary of Modern Egypt* (Cairo: The American University in Cairo Press, 2000), p. 57.

13 For more on the film, see Samir Farid, *Najib Mahfuz wa-al-sinima* (Cairo: al-Hay'a al-'Amma li-Qusur al-Thaqafa, 1990), p. 18. For details of Rayya and Sakina's crimes and their memorialization in a museum, see Rasha Sadeq, "The Other Citadel," *Al-Ahram Weekly*, February 20, 2003.

14 See Goldschmidt, *Biographical Dictionary*, pp. 234–35.

15 *Ibid*, p. 47.

16 Naguib Mahfouz, *Palace Walk*, translated by William M. Hutchins and Olive E. Kenny (Cairo: The American University in Cairo Press, 1989), p. 498.

17 To Atiyatallah Ibrahim Rizq, 25 years his junior, who bore him two daughters—Umm Kulthoum and Fatema (who prefer to be known as Hoda and Faten respectively).

18 Naguib Mahfouz, "Umm Ahmad" in collection *Sabah al-ward* (Cairo: Maktabat Misr, 1987), p. 7. Passage translated by this writer.

19 That this evidently never-realized relationship was in effect a dream was the observation of Shirley Johnston.

20 *Nisf al-dunya* magazine, Cairo, February 14, 1999. Translated by this writer.

❧ The Dreams ❧

Dream 1

I was riding my bicycle from one place to another, driven by hunger, in search of a restaurant fit for my limited means. At each one I found its doors locked, and when my eyes fell on the clock in the square I saw my friend at its foot.

He called me over with a wave of his hand, so I headed my bike in his direction. In view of my condition, he suggested that, in order to make my quest easier, I leave my bicycle with him. I followed his suggestion—and my hunger and my search grew even more intense, until I happened upon a family eatery.

Propelled by the need for food and by despair, I approached it, despite knowing how expensive it was. I saw the owner standing at the entrance before a hanging curtain. What could I do but to throw it open—only to find the place changed into a ruin filled with refuse in place of its grand hall readied with culinary delights. Dismayed, I asked the man, "What's going on?"

"Hurry over to the kabab-seller of youth," he answered. "Maybe you can catch him before he shuts down."

Not wasting any time, I ran back to the clock in the square— but found neither the bicycle there, nor my friend.

Dream 2

We entered the apartment, the girl in the lead and I right behind her, while the doorman carried our bags. The girl and I had a firm relationship—though it was somehow undefined. We had begun to arrange our things when I sauntered onto the balcony overlooking the sea, and became lost in its vague horizons, intoxicated by its broken roar and its humid breeze.

Suddenly a scream issued from inside the flat. I scurried toward it to find the girl convulsed in terror as flames licked through the top of the doorway. Before I could recover from the shock, a man with features so hard they seemed cut from stone came in and—with a wave of his hand—put out the fire.

"Maybe the water service here will be cut off for a while," he said, turning toward us—then went away.

My mind now at rest, I left my room for the supermarket to buy some needed things. Coming back, I discovered the apartment door open with the doorman standing around. I went into the flat, feeling anxious, and found it was bare but for a fat package of clothes tossed onto the floor. An arm from a pair of pyjamas stuck out through a hole in its wrapping. There was no trace of the girl.

"What's happened?" I wondered.

"You must have gotten mixed up, sir, on your way here—this is not your apartment," the doorman replied.

Staring at the protruding arm, I said, "Those pyjamas are mine!"

He replied calmly, "You'll find thousands like them in the shops."

I felt inclined to accept that I'd erred, especially in recalling that there were three buildings in a row that resembled each other here. Quickly I raced down the stairway to the street—and saw the girl walking through its emptiness toward the square jammed with people and with cars. I ran to catch up with her before she melted into the crowd.

Dream 3

At the center of the boat's deck was a mast. A man was bound to it by a rope that wrapped around him from his upper torso to his lower legs. He twisted his head violently both right and left, crying out from his wounded depths, "When will this torture end?"

Three of us looked toward him with sympathy, exchanging confused glances with each other. A voice asked him, "Who's doing this to you?"

The tormented man replied, as his head continued to thrash from side to side, "I'm the one doing it."

"Why?"

"This is the punishment I deserve."

"For what offence?"

"Ignorance," he said, sighing with anger.

"We knew you as one who had a dream, as well as experience," I answered him. "We did not know that rage lies latent in every person."

"You were also ignorant of the fact," he batted back, his voice rising, "that no human being can be stripped of all nobility, no matter how wretched their condition!"

At this, we were conquered by sadness and silence.

Dream 4

A huge, spacious hall, completely empty but with many doors. The three of us were standing in a hidden corner. My two friends strutted about like dandies, even wearing neckties, while I made do with a Moroccan *jellaba*—yet, thanks to our closeness as friends, I felt no embarrassment.

I heard a movement, and looked to see a man who came from I don't know where dressed in formal attire, suggesting that he was some sort of master of ceremonies. I wrapped my *jellaba* around myself and said to my two friends, "I'm afraid there's a party going on here!"

They replied, one after the other: "I don't think so."

"That's not important."

I became aware of another movement and when I looked I saw two men similar to the first joining him. At this point, all doubt vanished and I bolted to the nearest door. When I opened it, it was as if I found myself facing a barrier formed by the wall of the reception hall. I repeated this with every door, but all my attempts were frustrated like the first. So I went back to my two friends, insinuated myself between them, and hid myself there.

I was somewhat reassured, however, that the three men took no notice of us at all.

I watched the movements around us as the invitees poured in from every direction.

The place kept filling up without any of them even looking at us, for all had their eyes focused on one place. I felt compelled to do as they were doing, when suddenly a magnificent person with the look of a leader appeared, as the din of applause grew louder. Each time the man advanced a step, the clapping grew stronger. Yet, at the same time, they warned him against going toward the door that it appeared he was heading for. So I said to my two companions, "He'll open it to find the doorway blocked, with no escape."

Amid the growing cheers and the continued warnings, the man opened the door, then disappeared from view as he ducked inside.

Dream 5

I am walking aimlessly without anywhere in particular to go when suddenly I encounter a surprising event that had never before entered my mind—every step I take turns the street upside-down into a circus. The walls and buildings and cars and passersby all disappear, and in their place a big top arises with its tiered seats and long, hanging ropes, filled with trapezes and animal cages, with actors and acrobats and musclemen and even a clown. At first I am so happy that I could soar with joy. But as I move from street to street where the miracle is repeated over and over, my pleasure subsides and my irritation grows until I tire from the walking and the looking around, and I long in my soul to go back to my home. But just as I delight once again to see the familiar face of the world, and trust that soon my relief will arrive, I open the door—and find the clown there to greet me, giggling.

Dream 6

The telephone rang and the voice at the other end said, "Shaykh Muharram, your teacher, speaking."

I answered politely with a reverent air, "My mentor is most welcome."

"I'm coming to visit you," he said.

"Looking forward to receiving you," I replied.

I felt not the slightest astonishment—though I had walked in his funeral procession some sixty years before. A host of indelible memories came back to me about my old instructor. I remembered his handsome face and his elegant clothes—and the extreme harshness with which he treated his pupils. The shaykh showed up with his lustrous *jubba* and caftan, and his spiraling turban, saying without prologue, "Over there, I have dwelt with many reciters of ancient verse, as well as experts on religion. After talking with them, I realized that some of the lessons I used to give you were in need of correction. I have written the corrections on this paper I have brought you."

Having said this, he laid a folder on the table, and left.

Dream 7

What a stupendous square, crammed with people and cars! I stood on the station's sidewalk, waiting for the arrival of Tram Number 3. It was nearly sunset. I wanted to go home, even though no one waited for me there.

Evening fell, the darkness blotting the lights of the widely-spaced lamps, and loneliness seized me. I wondered what was holding up Tram Number 3? All the other trams came in, each carrying away those who had been waiting for it—yet I had no idea what had happened to Tram Number 3. Movement in the square diminished as traffic slowly ground to a halt, until I was left nearly alone in the station. I glanced around and noticed to my left a girl who looked like a daughter of the night. My sense of isolation and despair only increased when she asked me, "Isn't this the stop for Tram Number 3?"

I answered that it was, and thought of leaving the place—when Tram Number 3 quietly pulled into the station. The only people aboard were the driver and the ticket conductor. Something inside me told me not to get on—so I turned my back to it, staying that way until the tram had gone.

Looking about afterward, I saw the girl standing there. When she felt my eye upon her, she smiled and walked toward the nearest alley—and I followed her in train.

Dream 8

Approaching my flat, I found that both panels of the front door were open. This was most unusual. From inside came loud noises and echoes of people talking. My heart pounded in expectation of some evil, when I saw my dear ones smiling sympathetically. Yet just as I became fully aware of everything, the apartment was cleared of its contents, the furniture heaped at one end inside. At the same time, workmen of all different ages—wall painters, mortar mixers, and water carriers—bustled about. And so the plot had been carried out during my absence, while my question was lost in the air. . . . Was this coup deliberately executed when I was in such a state of complete exhaustion?

I shouted at the workmen, "Who told you to do this?" But they kept on doing their jobs without paying me any mind. Overwhelmed by anger, I stepped out of the flat—feeling that I would never go back into it as long as I lived. At the building's entrance I saw my mother coming, long after she had left this world. She seemed furious and indignant. "You're the cause of all this!" she said to me.

"No—you're the cause of what's happened here, and of the things to come!" I shot back.

Then quickly she vanished, and I continued my flight.

Dream 9

On the couch in the little garden attached to the house my sister sat staring contemplatively at a frog swimming in the canal that flowed through the greenery. As she did so, she grew intoxicated on the tender breeze and the clusters of grapes dangling from the trellis.

I asked my sister, "What are you waiting for?"

Before she could answer, I said, "It's better to sit inside where we can listen to the phonograph." We exchanged consulting looks, then went into the room. There the silence became more intense until even the breeze abandoned us.

I looked at my sister—and she had turned into the screen star Greta Garbo. She was my favorite actress, so I soared with happiness, though without any wings.

I trembled with pleasure, yet the enchantment was brief. I wanted to bring the miraculous magic back once again—but my sister refused to help. I asked her why she had said no.

"My mother . . . " she replied.

I cut her off before she could finish.

"She doesn't know," I told her.

"She knows everything," she declared confidently.

I felt that sadness had blanketed everything, like a sudden fog.

Dream 10

Our friendship and our growing up together have brought us all here. We have grown used to this alley, and, as the coattails of night come down upon us, we have no goal but to delight in our gathering and surrender to jesting and laughter, and to compete in the art of telling rhyming jokes to each other.

We trade our witty wisecracks as we turn little by little into ghosts in the gloom. We know each other by our voices, and do not pause in savoring our amusing competition. Our guffawing goes up against the four walls around us, waking those who are sleeping. The alley recedes as we draw closer to one another, while the darkness engulfing us fails to dissolve. As all of this happens, we continue as we were until confusion cramps our gaiety, and we begin to wonder if we might best finish our evening elsewhere—perhaps on a square, or on a main road.

One of us tells the story of the pharaonic queen who wanted to take revenge on the priests who had killed her husband. She invited them to a place very much like the one in which we are now rejoicing—then the waters overcame them. He has not quite finished his tale when the heavens open upon us with unprecedented force. The thunder stills us as the water pours down, rising until it covers our feet and creeps up our calves, and we feel that we are drowning in the rain in the shadow of night. We forget all of our jokes and all of our laughter.

In the end, there is no hope left for us—unless we fly into space.

Dream 11

In the shade of the date palm on the bank of the Nile, a girl of great height and succulent body lay upon her back. Her chest was open as countless children kept crawling toward her. They swarmed about her breasts and sucked from them with unimaginable greed. Each time one group of them finished, another would approach.

The whole thing appeared to have gotten out of hand, over-throwing any system of order. To me it seemed that someone should raise an alarm and call for help. Yet the people were shrouded in sleep on the Nile's shore. I tried to cry out, but no sound came from my mouth. My breast tightened with distress.

As for the children with the woman, they had left her nothing but skin over bones. When they despaired of getting any more milk from her, they tore at her flesh with their teeth until they had rent her to a mere skeleton. I felt it my duty to do more than just attempt the scream that I couldn't get out of me. It startled me that the children, after giving up on finding more milk and meat, had sunk into a beastly battle with each other. Their blood flowed as their flesh was torn.

Some of them caught sight of me and began to come toward me—to do the unthinkable in the infinity of total terror.

Dream 12

Something in the air afflicted the nerves. From several directions, heads would pop out—then as suddenly vanish. Rumors of conflict spread with the speed of shooting stars. The word "war" was repeated on every tongue.

Confusion and unease became widespread. I saw people hoarding essential supplies. In those worrisome days, I kept wondering—should we stay, or should we flee abroad? And then, where to?

I savored being in a safe place, sheltered from danger, when a man from the security apparatus came to me. Straight away, he said, "The State wants to know the ability of families who already have lodgings to take in those in need of shelter, God permitting."

Everywhere the troubles kept doubling. My mother, who lived by herself in a huge house, declared that she was prepared to take in a whole family—while I resolved to give up one room to accept two persons. Meanwhile, I grew wary of any sound or of answering any question. An informer came to my door and invited me to the station. When asked the reason for my summons, he told me nastily that he didn't know, before our converstion was cut off by the sound of the warning siren.

Dream 13

ere was the airport. Its atmosphere rumbled with sundry sounds and languages. The women, having finished all their procedures, stood waiting. I drew close to them, offering each one a rose in a silver wrapper.

"Travel safely—with prayers for your success," I said.

They thanked me, smiling, as one of them said, "This is a strenuous mission, and it will take years and years for us to succeed."

I grasped what she meant, and pain gripped my heart. We traded silent looks of farewell, as the old times passed before our eyes. The airplane moved: my vision followed it until the vessel vanished over the horizon. When I returned to the reception hall, all I could recall was my desire to find the post office.

It was if I had come with only this goal. I heard a voice whisper, "Do you want the post office?" Puzzled, I peered in its direction—to find a girl whom I had never seen before. I asked her who she was.

"I'm Rayya's daughter. Maybe you remember Rayya and Sakina?"

In mounting panic, I replied, "The memory frightens me!"

"If you want the post office," she advised, "then follow me."

So—with the fiercest trepidation—I did as she said.

Dream 14

I was walking along the green banks of the Nile. The night was damp as the secret dialogue continued between the moon and the river's waters, on which the luminous rays rippled. My spirit wandered through the recesses of Abbasiya, suffused with the scent of love and jasmine.

I found myself debating the question that had assailed me from time to time—why hadn't she visited me in a dream even once since she died, at the very least to confirm that she was real, and not merely an adolescent fantasy? Was her picture imprinted in my mind really a true likeness? Then, with the sound of music blaring from the direction of the darkened street, ghosts appeared, their forms solidified by the light of the first lamp they happened to approach. To my astonishment, the brass band was not strange to me—I had listened to it often in my youth, as it marched in the wake of funerals. This tune I almost knew by heart.

But the truly happy coincidence was the sight of my departed sweetheart walking behind the musicians: this was surely her, with her ravishing appearance, her sublime step, and her refined face. Finally she had blessed me with a visit. Leaving the burial procession, she stood in front of me to prove that life had not all been in vain. Standing breathlessly erect, I rushed toward her with all the strength of my soul, saying to myself that this chance—to touch the darling of my heart—would never come again.

Moving a step toward her, I took her in my arms—then heard the crackle of something breaking. Her dress felt as though it was draped over empty space—and no sooner had I discovered this, than the marvelous head fell to the ground and rolled into the river. The waves bore it away like a Rose of the Nile—leaving me to eternal grief.

Dream 15

A great hallway along which offices were arrayed. A government department, or perhaps a commercial agency. The employees were either sitting quietly at their desks, or moving about between their offices. They were made up of both sexes, obviously working well together, lightly and openly flirting with each other. I seemed to be one of the newer functionaries here, with a suitably low salary, a fact that I felt profoundly. Yet this didn't prevent me from asking for the hand of a beautiful young lady of higher rank, who had worked here longer than me. In the event, she thanked me, but declined my request.

"We lack what we'd need for a happy life," she explained.

This pierced me with a wound in the seam of my psyche.

From that day onward, I grew wary of broaching any such subject with my female colleagues, though I was attracted to more than one of them. I felt the bitter suffering of loneliness and dejection. Then a new girl joined our service—and for the first time, I found myself in a superior position. I was an auditor, while she was a typist: my salary was twice as large as hers. She was not good looking, and, even worse, people gossiped about her immoral behavior. Out of despair, I decided to break through my isolation—so I flirted with her. She flirted back. So happy was I that I lost my head and asked her to marry me.

"I'm sorry," she replied.

Not believing my ears, I pressed on, "There's nothing wrong with my salary, especially when added with yours."

"Money doesn't concern me," she said.

I thought of asking what *did* matter to her, but she'd already walked away.

Dream 16

The assisting doctor congratulated me on the operation's success. Awaking from the anaesthesia, I felt deep relief and happiness for my sheer survival. I'd gone into the recovery room, when a nurse came and sat on a chair, bringing her head close to mine. After staring at me thoughtfully for quite some time, she said with intense composure, "How long I've waited to see you lying weak and helpless like this."

I looked back at her and said with dismay, "But this is the first time I've seen you in my life—why would you wish me any harm?"

With malice and resentment, she replied, "The time for vengeance has come."

She stood up and left the room, leaving me in a vortex of perplexity, fear, and anxiety. How could this woman imagine I had ever done her ill, when I had never seen her before? The surgeon came to check on me. I clung to him, saying, "Doctor, please understand—my life is in danger!"

He listened as I told him what had happened. He ordered all the nurses serving in the ward to file in front of me—but the one I sought was not among them.

As he left, the doctor assured me, "You're under our complete protection here."

The evil forbodings did not forsake me. Everyone who entered the room peered at me strangely, as if I'd become an object of wonder and doubt—while I saw a long road full of hardships ahead.

Dream 17

The quarters of Gamaliya and Abbasiya passed before me, yet I seemed to be walking in only one place. I imagined that someone was tailing me. I turned to look behind me, but the rain poured down more intensely than it had in years—so I scurried back to my home. I wanted to take off my clothes, but then had the uncanny feeling that a strange man was hiding in my house. His audacity infuriated me—so I screamed at him to give himself up. The door to the foyer opened and there appeared a man whose equal in size and strength I had never before seen. "Give *yourself* up," he said, in a quietly sarcastic voice.

A sense of feebleness and fear gripped me: I was certain that one blow from his elephant-sized hand would flatten me completely. Then he ordered me to give up my wallet and my overcoat. The overcoat was more important to me—yet I hesitated but a little before handing him both items. He shoved me, and I hit the ground. When I regained my feet, he had disappeared—and I wondered if I should call out to raise an alarm.

But what had happened was contemptible and shameful, and would make me an object of jokes and ridicule—so I did nothing.

I thought about going to the police station, but one of my friends was an officer from the detective bureau. Hence the scandal would spread one way or another.

I decided upon silence, but this didn't save me from worry.

I dreaded that I would run into the thief somewhere while he was walking happily about in my coat, and with my money.

Dream 18

We sat on both sides of the launch. Each man appeared singly, with no relation to the others—then the pilot came and started up the boat's motor.

The pilot was a beautiful young girl. My heart quivered at the sight of her. She looked out of the window as I stood beneath the tree: the time was somewhere between childhood and the first stirrings of early manhood. I fixed my eye on her noble head as she speedily steered us along the river, my heart pounding in harmony with the gusts of the breeze. I thought of going up to her to see how she would receive me.

But then I found myself on a street in one of the poorer quarters—it might have been the Ghuriya—as it was jammed with humanity on the birth-feast of Husayn. I caught sight of her making her way with difficulty down one of the winding lanes, and resolved to catch up with her—while the group of chanting celebrants fêted the martyred saint.

Just as quickly I returned to my seat on the boat, which had covered a great stretch of the river. I glanced at the bridge, and saw that the pilot was an elderly woman with a brooding face. I looked around and wondered about the absent young beauty—and saw nothing but empty seats.

So I began to query the old hag about the missing, lovely girl.

Dream 19

I was dazzled by the new apartment after it was turned over to me. I inspected every corner—and it filled my soul with joy. "Now you need a regular job," I told myself. "You'd better get cracking without delay."

I went to the market. Covering a vast area, it was surrounded by a formidable wall. I presented my deed of ownership for the flat, and they let me come inside.

The place was packed with people. I saw a great many women I had loved in the past, but all were walking arm-in-arm with their men. I proceeded to the intended window and offered my papers, the first being my proof of possession for the new apartment. The man looked them over and told me, "We don't have any vacant positions right now. We'll get in touch with you at the appropriate time."

I felt my hopes frustrated—I would have to wait a long while. I returned to cutting my way through the crowd, contemplating the rush of gorgeous faces that I had loved before. I lingered alone in the flat, while on the street I heard a man say in a booming voice, "It's nonsense for a man to own an apartment without holding down a job. He should give it up for someone else fortunate enough to be employed."

I was upset by what he said—and the longer I thought about it, the truer it seemed.

Assailed by doubt and worry, I watched for what lay hidden behind the morrow with a troubled and sleepless eye.

Dream 20

We went out looking for a good place to pass the time. We gazed at the crescent moon, exchanging glances—and saw by the lamplight a giant whose like was never before seen by the human eye.

He threw a rod which had no equal in length toward the crescent, striking it squarely. With a brilliant movement it began to unroll its folds of light until it ripened into a full moon. We heard voices shout, "There is no god but God!" and we shouted it with them. I said that nothing like this had ever happened before, and she agreed. The light flowing over creation lifted me over the surface of the water. She called out, "A moonlit night!" and I said, "The boat is inviting us!" as we rode along with the utmost pleasure.

Then the pilot sang, *"I crave you, by the Prophet, I crave you."* We grew drunk with ecstasy, and I suggested that we swim around the skiff. We stripped off our clothes and leapt into the water, splashing about with absolute delight. But then the moon suddenly turned back into a crescent—and the crescent, too, disappeared. We grew alarmed as we never had before, and I felt that this required a serious reappraisal of our situation. With the two of us drowning in the dark, I said, "Let's head for the boat."

"And if we get lost?" she replied.

"We can make for the shore," I answered.

"We'll be naked on the bank," she fretted.

"Let's worry about that later," I told her.

Dream 21

On this little street there was no want of pedestrians out and about, or people sitting on their balconies. The lady walked slowly, sometimes stopping in front of the fashion displays.

Four young men, not yet twenty years old, made their way toward her. She frowned in their faces and turned away from their path. But they swooped down upon her, harassing her. She resisted them as the neighborhood watched without intervening. The youths tore her robe, exposing parts of her body, as the woman cried out in alarm. I observed what was happening and stopped in my tracks, paralyzed by shock and disgust. I wanted to do something—or wanted someone else to do something—but nothing occurred.

After the tragedy had finished and the criminals had fled, the police arrived, the place changed—and I found myself with a group of others in front of the officer's desk. Our testimony was all in accord. When asked what we did, we answered, "Nothing." I was embarrassed and disturbed, my hand trembling as I affixed my name to the official report.

Dream 22

We were working in the office when he looked me in the face and said, "Your mind is preoccupied."

I answered tersely, powerless with fatigue, "The cost of the medicines is beyond my means."

"I understand and appreciate that," he said, "and I praise God who saved me from its claws."

So I asked him, "How could you survive that for which there is no survival?"

He replied, "I have a friend whose brother is a pharmacist. When he knows that I have an illness, he assures me that he'll find a solution. He takes down what medications I and my family need each month, which he tells to his brother the druggist—then surprises me with their equivalent for less than a tenth of the regular price."

I asked him if these operations weren't dangerous. He tried to put me at ease, speaking to me at length on the ways of the different pharmaceutical companies until he had me upset and confused. Nonetheless, I didn't hesistate—but wrote for him a list of the medications that I needed each month, and felt deeply relieved.

Then suddenly he said to me, "But I want a service from you in return." I began to prepare myself to do what he asked.

"I'm disturbed by the attacks on the government's red tape and bureaucracy. The government is aggrieved by what people say and write on this subject—so I want you to devote your pen to defending against it." Astonished, I asked, what was the secret of his zeal for something that all people alike criticize and reject?

Angrily, he replied, "Brother, what is a civil servant worth who faces the public without bureaucracy and red tape?" My head whirled in confusion between the medications and the procedural maze.

Dream 23

I was strolling down the street. I knew this place well—for it was where I worked and where I played, where I met my friends and my sweethearts alike. I greeted this one as I shook hands with that one—while noticing a man crossing in front of me, neither very close nor very far away.

From time to time, he would turn about to be sure that I was behind him. Perhaps this wasn't the first time I'd seen him, but certainly there was no mutual bond between us. What he was doing annoyed me, and presented me with a challenge. I quickened my steps, and he quickened his. I felt he was plotting something, and this made me more defiant. Then a friend called me over to deal with some private business and I headed to his shop, where, absorbed in conversation, I forgot about the man.

When, in the late afternoon, our business was finished, I bid my friend goodbye. As I made for my house, I remembered the man and turned to look behind me. I saw him following me, just as I had found him walking ahead of me before. . . . Incensed, I decided to stop to see what he was doing. Instead, I found myself moving faster as though I were fleeing from him. Dismayed, I wondered, what does he want?

When my house came in sight, I finally felt relaxed as I opened the door and stepped inside without a glance over my shoulder. Finding the place empty, I went to my bedroom—then stopped at the peculiar sensation that the man was lurking within.

Dream 24

A fter not a short absence, I decided that my flat in Alexandria needed some repairs. The laborers came, the foreman at their lead. The work began with remarkable energy. My attention was drawn to a particular youth—who seemed strangely familiar. I felt a frisson in my body when I recalled that I had indeed seen him once—as he attacked a woman on a side street, taking her bag and running away. Yet I wasn't sure, so—without the boy's sensing it—I asked the foreman how much he trusted him.

"He's as bankable as a gold pound," the foreman said, "for he's my son, whom I've raised myself." This calmed my heart for a time—though whenever my sight fell on the boy my chest began to tighten. Seeking a sense of safety, I opened one of the windows that overlooked the street in which there labored those whom I knew and who knew me—but instead, I saw the alley of the garage on which my flat in Cairo looks down. Amazed, my heart pounded even more. As the time went on and darkness approached, I asked the men to end their work for the day before the evening began, since the electricity had been cut due to my long time away.

"Don't worry," the unsettling youth said, "I have a candle." Concerned that the situation would offer him an opportunity to steal whatever was light enough to carry, I went to look for the foreman—and was told that he had gone into the wash-room. Waiting for him to come out with mounting anxiety, I imagined that his disappearance into the W.C was part of a conspiracy—and that I was alone with a gang of thieves. I called out to the foreman as the signs of approaching evening spread through the flat.

Dream 25

She was in the room with me—and no one else. My heart danced, singing with joy. I knew that my happiness would be brief: it wouldn't be long before the door would open and someone would come in. I longed to tell her that I gladly accepted all the conditions that had been communicated to me, but that I would need at least a brief time to meet them. Yet, enchanted by her presence, I said nothing.

Seized by desire, I took two steps toward her—but then the door swung open. The professor came in. "You don't know the meaning of time," he told me sharply. I tore myself away and followed him to his institute, which was opposite our building. There he said to me, "You need to work ten hours a day until you perfect your playing." He commanded me to sit down to practice the piano, and soon I was engrossed in my labor—while my heart hovered about back in my room.

When I was granted leave, the evening was descending in all its glory. I set out to cover the route quickly, yet there was no hope that she would wait for me all through my absence.

Just then a man from China with a long beard and a smiling face blocked my path. "I was in the institute while you were playing," he said. "There's no doubt that a splendid future awaits you." With a bow in my direction, he left.

I continued on my way, shuddering at the thought of the loneliness that attended me where I lived.

Dream 26

We met in my local café, where my friend read to us a detective story he had written. Nearing the end, he asked us to guess the killer's identity—and who had paid him to commit the crime. I ventured the right answer—which made me incredibly glad.

After an hour, I excused myself to go home. But success had made me so euphoric that I wandered through the streets until, eventually, I found myself back in front of the café, which made everyone laugh. One of them volunteered to escort me to my house, and when we arrived there he said goodbye and left. My house was built in one story, set in a little garden. I felt like taking off my clothes, and when I was down to my underwear, I noticed a streak of dust projecting downward from one of the room's corners. That same image was found in the story my friend had read to us—it was a warning that the house would fall down on whoever was inside.

I wept that my little place was going to collapse on my head. In the grip of terror, I fled for safety as far and as fast as the wind would take me.

Dream 27

On a ship crossing the ocean, people of all colors and tongues were arrayed. We were expecting the wind to swoop down, and when it did, the horizon disappeared behind the angry waves. I became frightened: it was every man for himself. I felt alone in the depths of the sea. An inner fear told me there was no way to survive the all-encompassing terror—unless this really was just a nightmare, to be shattered by a fevered awakening on my bed.

The wind became violent as the boat was tossed back and forth on the waves. Suddenly, I saw before me Hamza Effendi, my math teacher, wielding his wicker rod. He fixed me with a look demanding to know if I had done my homework. If I hadn't, he would rap me ten times across my knuckles—which made them feel as though they'd been pressed with a hot iron. My hatred grew with the memory of those days.

I wanted to grab him by the neck, but feared that any move would cause my demise. So, saying nothing about my humiliation, I swallowed it despite the dryness in my throat. I saw my sweetheart and scurried toward her, cutting my way through tens of confused onlookers. But she did not recognize me and turned her back, proclaiming her annoyance. Then she ran toward the ships's edge and threw herself into the storm—I thought she was showing me the way to deliverance. So I rushed stumblingly toward the side of the ship, but the old math teacher stood in my path, brandishing his stick of bamboo.

Dream 28

The wheel turned and turned, and the money came and went, as the young beauty served the drinks, and sometimes sandwiches, too. Then fortune smiled on me and I won a good sum of pounds, which seemed immense in our limited world.

Feeling slightly dizzy, I announced that I would withdraw—yet no one believed my reason for doing so. As I was leaving, one of the players accused the girl of revealing what cards they held. She grew furious—as did I—in reaction to this baseless charge. The accuser stood up, along with two others, tearing the girl's clothes until she was practically naked. All the while, she screamed and threatened to inform the police about the apartment, where gambling and other forbidden things were going on. At this, they all returned quickly to their seats, as I helped the girl back into her clothes—then departed for my own apartment nearby.

I had just sat down to relax when the girl came to see me. She said the group was angry and that drunkenness had made them even angrier—they were threatening to storm my house and create an uproar in the whole quarter. She advised me to return my winnings as a solution to the problem. I argued that they would consider that a confession to a crime we had not committed. She replied that was less heinous than what they intended to do—so I deferred to her point of view, giving her the money. She took it and left.

The serenity of night returned—but I continued to expect a scandal or some other evil.

Dream 29

The place was new to me—I had not seen it before. Perhaps it was the grand salon of a hotel where the Harafish used to sit together around a banquet table. They were talking about the choice of the best female writer of renown. It seemed clear that the woman I had nominated would not be accepted. They said she was only superficially cultured and her behavior was depraved.

Playfully, I tried to defend her, when I noticed they were looking at me with unprecedented grimness, as though they had forgotten our lifelong intimacy. I got up to leave the salon, but none of them stirred, as they all glared at me, seething with rage.

I walked toward the elevator and stepped into it, nearly on the verge of tears. Then I became aware of a woman in the lift with me—her face was severe, and she was dressed like a man. She told me that she mocked what they call friendship: the way people dealt with each other had to change drastically. While I thought about the meaning of all this, she pulled a pistol from her pocket and pointed it at me, demanding any cash that I had with me. It was all over quickly, and when the elevator came to a stop and the door opened, she ordered me to get out.

As the lift resumed its descent, I found myself in an unlit corridor. Overwhelmed with the feeling that I had lost my friends, I feared that incidents like this robbery were waiting out there to ambush me, wherever I should go.

Dream 30

This was our house in Abbasiya. I went into the salon. My mother walked toward the entrance as my sister approached. My sister stopped for a few moments before joining her. We didn't greet each other, but I declared my intense hunger in a loud voice. No one replied, so I repeated my demand.

I heard voices in the room overlooking the field, so I went toward it, discovering my oldest brother sitting in silence. Across from him, the Shaykh of al-Azhar sat cross-legged on the couch. The shaykh was speaking beautifully. When he finished, I told him I was hungry. He retorted that no one had served him coffee, or even a glass of water. I left the room and said—in a voice that my mother and sister would hear—that someone should bring coffee to His Eminence the Shaykh. But I heard only silence, except for the phonograph and the recordings that I adored—and I found the neighbors' daughter who would visit me to borrow some records, especially that of Sayyid Darwish, which I loved the most. She was looking for a needle with which to play the record.

I told her I was hungry, and she said that she was hungry, too. My hunger overcame me and I went out of the room and called out, begging for a bite of something! Finding nothing, I left the house as evening shaded the empty street. Fearing that all the shops were closed, I made for the bakery—faint with starvation, yet enticed by hope.

Dream 31

A donkey carried me through the midst of the fields with monotonous steps, stripped of any feeling under the rays of the autumn sun. A dog's barking hailed us, and the donkey halted. I prodded him with my heel and he resumed his gait.

The barking and wailing returned, and I screwed up my vision to scan for the man I was seeking. A woman appeared, surrounded by a pack of dogs. She shouted at them to keep quiet, and they obeyed. I greeted her and said that I had come to meet the shaykh, on the basis of two letters we had exchanged. The woman replied that she was the person ultimately in charge of this matter and that she was able to offer the requested services—just as she was able to annihilate whomever she wished, if she set the dogs upon them.

I answered that I had come in peace, not war, and I wanted work. She motioned toward me, and I came down from the donkey's back, standing before her in submission. She walked, and I followed, the donkey trailing behind me, with the dogs all around us. She stopped in front of a small building, and the whole procession stopped with her. She commanded me to go inside: I entered, and she said that I should wait within. She warned of the dogs that would show no mercy if I ventured outside. I asked her how long I would have to comply—and what about my job? The shaykh, I pointed out, had promised me a good turn. She paid no heed to what I said, but mounted the donkey and rode away, leaving the dogs encircling my prison.

She has been sending me the things I need through tough-looking men, who never say a word. Sometimes I think of taking on the dogs in a battle of life or death, but hope is triumphant.

And I wait.

Dream 32

My old colleague let me know that he was going to work in Yemen. He added there was a rumor that I, too, had been invited to work in Yemen—and urged me to accept it. I promised to think about it without showing any enthusiasm.

Yet in the house where I lived by myself, with only my female dog for company, I began to think about the matter in an unexpected manner. What caused this was my sudden aversion to my dog, after her face had started to change into that of a human being. Before this happened, she was my attractive and amusing canine. But after the confusing transformation, she was no longer my dog—nor was she quite human.

Then instantly I found myself in my office in Yemen, my male private secretary standing in front of me. The heat was intense, so I asked the secretary about the type of weather found in this country. He said that it was warm in winter and very hot the rest of the year—but the building was very tall, and the higher up you went, the more the weather would improve. Indeed, whenever the weather bothered me, I should write a memorandum to the director asking to transfer my office to a higher floor. I felt good after my earlier irritation, and—looking up—the building seemed so extremely huge, I imagined it actually touched the heavens.

Heads peered out of windows high up—and my heart pounded when I saw they bore the faces of those I loved in my earliest days. I felt an unsurpassable pleasure, praising God that I had accepted the offer to work in Felicitous Yemen.

Dream 33

What had happened to the street, and to the whole quarter? Whatever it was, I didn't expect anything good from what I saw.

The quarter looked completely decrepit with age. Its splendor gone, garbage was strewn here and there. I came across a laborer, and asked him, "What's going on?"

"Only God lasts forever," he said, smiling. "God be praised, all things change."

I headed for my friend's residence, expecting that what happened to the quarter would have befallen it, too, or even worse. I wouldn't deny he was my go-between for getting some medicines I needed from abroad, just as his telephone call could solve the most intractable problems in government offices. I found him depressed and without hope, so I consoled him. "In any case," I said, "at least you have a profession."

"The passing days will prove that we are not worse off than anyone else," he replied derisively.

I asked myself, is there truly anything worse? No sooner had I said this, then a group of young men and women appeared. Each one carried a bag full of things from the apartment— pyjamas and underclothes, alluring ladies' blouses, cosmetic creams, and perfumed fragrances.

Each one left, carrying his bag . . . Each item spoke of what kind of services had been offered in my friend's flat—as it testified to his decline.

I wondered, is he really doing so well, or is he miserable with humiliation and remorse?

Dream 34

On one of the winding lanes of our quarter, I ran into two friends who were brothers: their long absence had saddened me greatly. Speechless for a moment, we threw our arms open wide and grasped each other warmly about the neck, as we recalled the griefs, the joys, and the beautiful nights of our distant past.

The two of them asked to visit my house, so I went with them toward it from a distance of some meters. They scrutinized room after room, laughing a long time, as was their custom, before expressing their regrets at the simplicity of the shelter—while mocking me with their burning, beguiling tongues. They asked what I did for a living. I told them I was a *rabab* player who sang about the travails of life and the betrayals of time, then performed some music for them.

"This is a beggar's life!" they scolded me—and hence weren't surpised when weakness and despair showed on my face.

They told me that they had been looking for me for a long time until they found me, and their concern for me had clearly not been misplaced. Yet now, they added, they had brought the good news of my imminent release from this suffering.

I praised God, then asked what this good news could be. They explained that soon I would emigrate with them to the gorgeous place of abundance and plenty. I asked, how could that be possible? They replied that, as I knew, they enjoyed a close connection to influential persons—and nothing good comes to you except through influential persons.

They then took me by the arm and walked me outside, where we met a man whose appearance and manner proclaimed he was someone of importance. He listened to the tale with a neutral expression, before saying that—for me—emigration would entail great dedication and enduring patience. He promised me a positive outcome, however, and my two friends sought to reassure me, as well.

Finally, the man said, "Wait for me at the mosque at the crack of dawn."

Dream 35

In our house in Abbasiya, we were all going to sleep when the voice of my brother's son awakened me.

"The roof's on fire!" he shouted.

I arose in terror as my nephew brought a wooden ladder. We put it up in the salon and each of one of us mounted it, everyone carrying as much water as he could to throw on the fire running between the corners. I burst into my sister's room and jarred her from her deep slumber: amazingly, she got up lazily, complaining that I never, ever let her savor her sleep. In any case, she helped us fill the buckets with water until we brought the fire under control.

We had begun to look for what caused the combustion when, in response to our neighbors' call for help, the men of the fire brigade arrived. Opening up the balconies to inspect the furniture we had shoved onto them, they confirmed the fire had indeed died out. The disaster had come to an end—after dumbfounding us with fear.

But just as we sat down to regain our composure, the telephone rang. Here one must note the change of time and place—for our house in Abbasiya did not have a telephone. Hence we were in another home with other people altogether. On the phone was the owner of the building where we rented our apartment in Alexandria. He urged us to come without delay, for fire had broken out in our place there. He reassured us that he had called in the fire brigade and they had subdued the blaze, but naturally our presence was nonetheless needed.

Immediately my wife and I got dressed and hurried to the station for the busses taking the Desert Road north. By this time, we were so distressed and confused that I suggested to my wife that we empty the flat of our belongings and turn it back to its owner, especially as there had already been an attempted robbery there.

But she told me to wait until we saw what was lost in it—and what still remained.

Dream 36

We were assembled in some sort of great hall. Then some faces appeared that I was seeing for the first time, as well as others that I knew very well that belonged to my colleagues. We were awaiting the announcement of what Fate had decreed.

The results were revealed, and I was the winner: the prize was a new, modern-style villa. There followed a tumult of comments and congratulations. Many faces were unable to conceal their sadness. Quite a few said that it was a win, all right, but also a misfortune—for where would I get the money to furnish it and pay the necessary staff, as well as to cover the water and electrical bills, to maintain the swimming pool, the air conditioning, and so on?

In truth, my dream was still but a dream: I inspected the villa nearly every day, only to meet disappointment and distress. People took advantage of my lack of experience and persuaded me to sell the place at a particular price. For an hour or so, I gleefully rejoiced at what I had gained—until it dawned on me that I had been had.

At that time, it happened that the post of general director in the civil service fell vacant. There were many candidates, some of whom had great connections, jostling madly to fill it. I met with the minister, telling him that he was my only point of influence in this affair. But he replied, "You aren't even able to protect your own money—so how could you be trusted with everyone else's?"

I became a peculiarity, an example of what not to be for my fellow employees. Finally, I asked that my remaining time in service be added to that already served, and to go on pension at once. At last, I felt the security of a position to which no one ever aspires out of greed, and which does not attract the eyes of the covetous.

Dream 37

The *mahmal* wobbled atop the camel, festooned with many colors and bouquets of flowers. Leading it was a man holding a pole upright in his mouth, bangles dangling from the pole's head.

The camel's head was at the level of the first floor of the house from where I watched through the window. My eye met the camel's own, and within his eye I read a smile and an *esprit* that placed a blessing within me. Suddenly, I flew from my spot behind the window and spun toward the camel's head, dressed in my *gallabiya*, my hair blown about. The people shouted, "God is most great!" and "There is no god but God!" and cried out incoherently at the sight of my feat. All the while, I kept rising in the air, until I landed on the roof of my house.

After the *mahmal* had passed, the people all flocked in front of my home, demanding to see the boy who could fly. They then turned abruptly from joyous amazement to fearful alarm, saying that an evil spirit possessed the levitating child—meaning me—and that his flight around the camel's head was an evil omen for all humanity. Therefore he must be freed of the Devil by flogging until he is cleansed completely. If he should refuse, then he would face the appropriate punishment—which was death.

Filled with fear, the lad and his family called in the police. The police chief demanded to see the miracle take place under his own eyes. He went to the house and witnessed the prodigious feat, and was truly dazzled by it. Yet he found himself torn between two points of view. The family claimed it was a wonder such as those performed by the saints—while the people denounced it as one of Satan's pranks, and a portent of misfortune.

Finally, the police chief decided to put the boy in prison until the whole subject was lost in oblivion.

Dream 38

I was sitting in my room, listening to a song on the phonograph, when a ravishing, elegant, and exciting woman of about twenty walked through the open door. Swept away by surprise and desire, I stood up and walked toward her until I stood in front of her.

Calmly she put out her hand, which held a letter. I took it and looked at it, then replied that I could not read it due to the weakness of my eyes, and asked her to read it for me. But she apologized that she did not know how to read or write, saying that her father had composed it for the prince whose name was found on the envelope. Before he died, her father had advised her to bring the missive to me so that I might deliver it to the prince for her. My astonishment mounting, I told her that I didn't know the prince in question—or any other prince, for that matter. I grew suspicious of her, and tried to change the subject, but then she left.

As I crossed the Qasr al-Nil bridge on my way to work, she appeared before me at the other end. I ignored her, but she followed me for not a short distance.

Coming back to my home, I discovered her quite settled in there. I warned her not to return to the subject of the letter. A long while passed, but still I wasn't free from evil forebodings—nor, clearly, was she. Definitely, we both had to flee by one route or another.

Dream 39

I stepped into the minister's room carrying a typewritten report bearing the names of the employees who had been nominated for promotion. My own name was among them. Obviously, the minister looked after me with special care. The minister having signed the declaration at the top, I took it to the personnel office for action. I went straight to the official in charge, who turned out to be a beautiful young woman. Looking at the document, she noted that the minister should have put his signature at the bottom, rather than the top. Hence it was impossible to execute the orders for promotions or to give raises to those listed on it. I became exasperated and complained of the bureaucracy that we had to put up with. Nonetheless, she stuck to her position—and I brought the report back to the minister. He signed it in the correct location, laughing as he did. I returned to the young woman, handing her the declaration. Sitting to the right of her desk was a female employee friend of hers known for her cheerfulness. The friend defended what her colleague had done, saying she was withholding promotion from the unmarried employees because she believed the rights of the married ones took precedence over theirs.

The first female employee pretended she was annoyed by the broadcast of this secret. When the happy-go-lucky one met me again afterwards, she asked my opinion of the official in personnel. I told her honestly that she had delighted me, so she suggested that I inform her of my feelings by way of introduction to a proposal of marriage. I asked for time to think it over—but she said I was no longer a young man, and that my life was being wasted on mere reflection.

She insisted that I tell her—so I surrendered, and did not refuse.

Dream 40

In the early evening I was returning to my house wrapped in a coat and scarf, when a young boy and an extraordinarily lovely and miserable girl cut across my path. They asked me for a bit of God's charity, so I searched in my pocket for some change. Not finding any, I pulled out a five-pound note and asked the boy to go to the nearest kiosk and buy me a piece of chocolate—and to keep whatever was left over.

The boy had no sooner left my sight when the girl began to weep, confessing that her brother treated her with great harshness and forced her to do bad things, and that every day these became more and more deviant and evil. She beseeched God to rescue her from her ordeal.

I felt moved and embarrassed, but then realized that the boy was not coming back. I saw how stupid I was to have placed any trust in him—and thought of how my family would accuse me of good-natured wrecklessness. Yet I did not leave his sister to him, but took her to my house to begin a new life with my family. Her situation so improved that she seemed more like one of us than our servant.

Then one day a policeman came, accompanied by the girl's brother, who grabbed her on sight. I found that I was wanted at the police station—where I was faced with a charge of raping the girl and keeping her in my home by force. I was shocked by what confronted me, and asked the girl to speak. She cried and accused me of crimes I had never even imagined.

The official report recorded every word as the world grew black before my eyes.

Despite my firmly-rooted faith, the danger of my position did not escape me.

Dream 41

The apartment broker said to me, "Don't get upset and don't despair—you have to be patient: patience is a virtue."

I knew that he knew the secret of my agony—that I was in danger of losing my home and finding myself on the street. I told him that I had seen a number of places that appealed to me, but always they were beyond my means. And what about these empty flats, whose value is appraised at a million pounds each? Amazingly, he confirmed that four of my female colleagues owned some of these vacant dwellings: he envied them their fantastic wealth.

The last hope, he informed me, was in the building of al-Hagg 'Ali in the Husayn district—but we had to wait for his return from Mecca. I told him that I remembered, from the days when we lived in the ancient quarter, that I myself used to buy *fuul* from him sometimes. The man laughed, pointing out that's what many people claim when they want to buy an apartment in his brand new building.

"He's the last hope," I remarked with fear.

Striking an encouraging tone, the broker repeated, "You have to be patient: patience is a virtue."

Dream 42

The ship cut its way through the stately waves of the Nile. We were sitting in a circle, in the center of which reposed our teacher. Clearly we were taking the final exam, and our answers were rated excellent. We dispersed for tea and cake. In the meantime, we received our diplomas.

The ship pulled up at the pier and we disembarked, each one bearing his degree in a giant envelope. I found myself walking down a wide street devoid of both people and buildings, when a lonely mosque loomed before me. I went toward it in order to pray and relax for a while, but when I went inside, it seemed to actually be an old house. I felt the urge to go back out, but a bunch of brigands surrounded me, taking my certificate, my watch, and my wallet, and raining a hail of blows upon me before disappearing into the recesses of the place.

I ran outside onto the street, not believing that I had survived. After walking a short way, I came across a patrol of policemen, and told their commander what had happened to me.

We all marched together to the house full of thieves. They rushed in with their weapons drawn—only to find it was a mosque where people were praying behind their imam. Confused, we beat a hasty retreat, and the patrol's commander ordered that I be placed under arrest.

I kept testifying over and over to what had befallen me, swearing the most sacred oath that it was true. But clearly they had begun to doubt my sanity—and I was no less perplexed than them.

Dream 43

The night of my paternal cousin's wedding, which was being held in our house in Abbasiya, amidst drums and songs. My cousin came forward arm-in-arm with his bride, both in their wedding clothes. Before they mounted the stairs to go into their married home, a police inspector cut them off. We all became confused and ask ourselves, "What's behind all this?"

The inspector swooped down on the bride, closely inspecting her face, taking her fingerprints on a little pad. He examined them with a magnifying glass—then put her under arrest and walked her over to the police car. Everyone realized what that meant, and gathered around my cousin, consoling him and praising God for having saved him from an impending evil.

Despite all that, the young man went away crying. I resolved to spend the night with my family in the house in Abbasiya, but discovered that all the electric lights had failed. I asked my sister how they managed to live in the dark. I also discovered that the walls needed painting and repair. I grew annoyed with the place, and wanted to fix it up and restore it to its splendor of old.

Dream 44

I found myself seated before the Minister of the Interior at his desk. A few days earlier, he had been my colleague in the newspaper: his selection as minister came as a surprise. I seized the opportunity to ask him for a meeting, and he received me with welcome and affection. Then I presented him with my request, to recommend me to a businessman known to be his friend, when I applied for a position in one of his companies.

He wrote out the requested letter by hand, and the meeting ended on a happy note. On the evening of the same day, as I promenaded on the banks of the Nile, a man whose name is bantered in the press accosted me. He pulled out a gun and robbed me of my money—roughly fifty Egyptian pounds.

Traumatized, I went back to my flat, yet took no action that would affect the appointment that the businessman had given me. The next morning, I was at his office. After a few minutes, he permitted me to enter. I handed him the reference, then froze where I stood.

"My Lord," I said to myself, in this moment of high anxiety—for he was the very thief who had robbed me, or his twin brother. The ground spun before me.

Dream 45

My motor boat raced across the surface of the lake, with another boat following me, or so I imagined. As I sped up, so did the other.

I felt assailed by panic: Why was he pursuing me? Nearing a great quay, I cast anchor and climbed the stairs onto a wide deck—which, I noticed, belonged to the Russian Embassy. The deck was filled with mourners who had come to give their condolences at the death of a dearly departed woman.

I greeted the ambassador, then took a seat, listening to what was being said about the deceased lady. I gazed at the lake. Seeing no trace of the boat that been trailing me, I felt relieved.

When the time was right, I got back in my boat and steered it toward the other shore. Looking behind me, I saw the strange skiff cruising in my wake. When I reached the lake's center, I saw it was better to head for shore than return to the embassy. At the shore, I told myself, the true situation would become clear—and I could confront it with all my strength.

Dream 46

We were gathered in a garden. As usual, our host was singing as we listened enraptured, sending up shouts of passion and approval. This disturbed the neighbors, who complained to the police. We saw the police coming and split up, trying to get away.

I ran in the previously agreed direction—and each time I looked behind me I saw a policeman running after me, as hard and as determined as I was myself. At the same time, it seemed there was someone running ahead of me as though in flight from me. Who could this person be?

The trim, comely figure reminded me of my absent girlfriend, which spurred me to run even faster. The policeman wanted to overtake me, while I wanted to escape him and catch up with my sweetheart. Thus we climbed the tower and ran up to its roof as I panted to embrace my darling—but then she leapt over the wall and plummeted to the ground from its height. I went out of my mind, and—my misery mounting—I jumped from the wall after my beloved as the policeman approached.

Hitting the ground like a bomb, I expected to feel the most horrendous pain—yet all was well. Completely unhurt, I stood up. Glancing around me, I found no sign of my girlfriend. Then I looked up to see the policeman leering down from the tower, drowning in laughter.

Dream 47

A group of boys were playing on the road just ahead of me: I felt they harbored some sort of ill will against me. This surprised me, for nothing to provoke that sentiment had ever occurred between us. As I walked on cautiously, I remembered with wonder the way I was at their age.

A huge shop loomed before me, which I took to be for selling pastry, as it said on its giant sign. The labor of preparation was at its most intense as I approached, asking: "Do the pastries you offer include baklava and *kunafa*?"

The men stopped their work to stare at me. At the same time, the gang of boys laughed boisterously and whistled. From the farthest corners of the shop, a man appeared and inquired, "Is it true there are still people who love baklava and *kunafa*?"

I strolled among the workers as the boys danced and whistled and thrust their clenched fists in my face.

Dream 48

I found the Harafish in the room when I arrived. I asked about the only one of us who was absent. They said they'd dispatched him to ask the great composer Sayyid Darwish to send the new ballet troupe along.

I hadn't realized how spoiled the atmosphere had grown between us, as their faces all scowled at me. I wanted to go away—but at that moment the ballet troupe arrived, enveloped in music and dance. The tension between us lessened as we threw ourselves into the dancing and singing. Raptures raining down on us, our hearts became purified—love and affection pervading us all.

As we reveled with the male and female dancers and chanted in chorus with the hymns and songs, we all made a silent covenant to record the history of that night.

Dream 49

I was heading toward the elegant white building. In the heart of the great hall, the beautiful woman was sitting. We held a meeting with her, and she began to talk about the artistic production company that she had decided to form.

We all welcomed the company and its owner, presenting our individual views about work and production. We differed on nothing—except the salaries. She proposed setting each person's salary by agreement with her. Some others thought the salaries should be based on a fixed percentage of the expenditures for films and plays. The debate carried over into the next session. I advised my colleagues that to stick to her idea would simply put us at her mercy: the percentage concept clarified the matter, shutting the door on any sort of opportunism.

The lady invited us to dinner, along with some other guests. After the meal, there was a celebration with music. Before we knew it, the woman had stripped off all her clothes and was dancing for us totally naked—an extremely enticing scene.

My final opinion was settled, once and for all: I resolved to distance myself completely from the company—and from its owner, as well.

Dream 50

I was staring at a seductive woman as she walked down the street, when he boldly came up and whispered in my ear. "If you have any orders," he said, "she's at your command." Despite the repulsive gleam in his eyes, I did not turn away. We agreed on a fee, one-half of which he demanded in advance: I gave him the half. He gave me an appointment, but when I showed up, I found him alone. He offered the excuse that she was indisposed, and he was perfectly prepared to repay the advance—but I believed him, leaving it with him.

He went on accosting me in my comings and goings, pleading for my patience. Fearing our encounters would damage my reputation, I informed him that my desire had since dampened. And—while I wouldn't demand the return of my down payment—he had to stay away from me. He stopped approaching me, but still kept showing up most places I would go.

Finally, I became fed up, hating him so much that I decided to move to Alexandria. At Sidi Gaber station, I saw him, standing there as though in waiting.

Dream 51

The train came to a stop, though there was no station. My lady companion asked why this had happened, but I didn't know how to answer her.

Next, squadrons of soldiers from the army encircled the train, then burst inside, wielding their guns. Many military officers who had been on the train, plus a certain number of civilians, were driven outside. I was among those placed under arrest, leaving my girlfriend distraught and afraid. We found ourselves out in the desert. The armed soldiers ordered us to remove our clothes except for our underwear. Then they moved the military detainees to one side and the civilians to another. We began to whisper to each other that we were lost and that the end had come.

The soldiers' commander came and called out to each of us by name. A voice among us asked, "Will you kill us without trial?"

The commander answered with candor, "There's no need here for a trial."

The train pulled away—and I remembered the one with whom I had come.

Dream 52

We were invited to a meeting in the Azbakiya Gardens. There it was suggested that we honor our glorious professor on the occasion of the hundreth anniversary of his birth. No one showed any enthusiasm—nor did anyone appear to object.

The ceremony, it was agreed, would take place in the Foreign Ministry, where he spent the flower of his life, and accomplished his greatest deeds. On the appointed day, I went early to inspect the place, immediately heading to the chosen hall. It was as elegant and awe-inspiring as always, though this time it was made even more glamorous by the presence of hundreds of gorgeous women the man had loved throughout his life.

They came dressed in identical uniforms for their role as hostesses, each one displaying the succulent splendor of youth. My heart pounded madly as I grew woozy amidst the charms of the raving beauties—succumbing to the lure of love. I simmered with the thoughts that I would utter in the speech conferring honor.

Dream 53

I inquired about my friend, and was told that the great musician and songwriter, Shaykh Zakariya Ahmad, chanted his tunes each night in his house until dawn. "What good fortune!" I exclaimed, and was invited to come by one evening.

I went into the vast room, whose walls were embellished with arabesques, and saw Shaykh Zakariya seated on a couch, cradling his 'ud. He sang, "*Would that please God?*" as his family—women and children—sat in a circle around a man hanging by his feet.

Beneath the man's head, but an arm's length away sat a great vat of acid.

I became confused.

My confusion was compounded when I realized that everyone present was following the songs, paying not the slightest heed to the man being tortured.

Dream 54

In the closed room, the discussion went on between the lady broadcaster and myself about local versus foreign music. At different points in the conversation, I stood at the piano and played some songs.

Every so often, the door would open and a woman from the household—she might have been my mother or someone else of her stature—would enter to offer drinks. Without doubt, she regarded our seclusion with suspicion. Tired of her surveillance, I decided to challenge it by doing the unexpected. So, when next I heard the door opening, I rushed toward the broadcaster and clutched her to my chest.

I saw nothing wrong or unusual in what I had done. When I had finished my act of defiance, the woman had not only disappeared from the room, but from the house entirely.

Dream 55

The debate raged between a man, a woman, and her five sons about the right of the mother— who had passed her sixtieth year—to enjoy life and love.

The argument pierced the walls and became the talk of all the neighbors.

Some said it was a spurious love between an old woman and a young man the same age as her children, who was greedy for the money she'd inherited from her late husband. Others declared that a person must accept whatever they get from life—and especially, from love—even if the price be high. The affair seemed a disaster to the woman in the eyes of her five sons. They wound up murdering their wayward mother and going to the dock for it—accused of planning the crime and carrying it out together. In the investigation, arguments raged whose recurrent themes were motherhood and filial piety, honor and dignity, reputation, and respect for traditions.

I still can recall their faces and their words. Just as I remember the deceased woman when she defied the years and the wagging tongues to go her own way—so dazzlingly, seductively dressed and perfumed.

Dream 56

I left the great house in which we had waited—each man alone, not knowing the others—and felt something like security after unease.

Yet the sense of relief didn't last long, for soon I imagined that others were following me. I glanced behind me and saw in the distance a group coming after me, gesturing with their hands in the breeze.

I quickened my pace until I broke into a run. On the road I spied the house to which I'd been invited, and instantly hurried toward it. I found the people there as if they were returning from abroad, organizing their things and dusting them off. None of them seemed surprised at my appearance among them. They stared at my face with such affection in their expressions, in their talk, and in their smiles, it was though I'd just come back with them from their travels.

For that moment, at least, I forgot about the people creeping up behind me.

Dream 57

I walked around the fort twice—a citadel of stone whose windows were like tiny holes. From each window appeared a face that I not only knew, but adored. Some had been traveling a long while; others had departed our world at different times. I stared with passion and grief—and imagined that each one was begging from its depths for me to set them free. After looking hopelessly at the stone fort's gate, I went to the authorities to ask for help.

I left them feeling satisfied, clutching a pole made of steel, and returned to the fort. I brandished the pole, and the faces peered out as I struck a mighty blow at the door, which split apart and collapsed. The faces vanished from the windows as shouts of joy and pleasure rose up, and I stopped, my heart beating hard—waiting to meet the dear ones with longing and desire.

Dream 58

Finally the new tram came to us, becoming the pearl of public transport in the Abbasiya quarter—and I was among the first to grow to hate it. At the start, I was attracted by its green and white color, by its decorated walls and its huge, plush seats. I sat upright marveling at its beauty, saying to myself this is a gorgeous museum, not a tram. But I noticed over time that the behavior of its passengers was far below the standard set by its elegance.

Truly I witnessed outrageous things. Once I saw a foreign boy pounce upon a little girl, wanting to devour her, but I thrust myself between them, reminding him that she was only a child. Before he could start fighting with me, a beautiful woman of middle age climbed aboard, as he shouted out, "I love you!" She told him that she had just returned from Europe where she had attended the party for the release of her autobiography.

She showed us a copy. On the cover was a picture of a totally naked woman!

Dream 59

His great height was amazing—and so was his behavior. His stature was like that of the minaret at our local mosque. As for his actions, he would block the path of anyone he chose among the people of our quarter, angling down from his lofty altitude until he stood face to face with them.

He would stare piercingly at their features, searching for their hidden secret. He would keep doing this, then bolt out of sight behind a bend in the road. People would encounter him with dumb surprise and intense dismay—until one of them trailed him to discover the secret of his mystery. When the man failed to come back after a long time, a group of the neighbors went out to search for him and make sure he was all right.

The shaykh of the *hara* then came to search as well, as was his duty, but returned with wounded pride. The affair wound up on every tongue, as ideas and fantasies multiplied in peoples' minds. Yet to no avail, for forgetfulness swallowed the whole business—or nearly so.

One evening the shaykh was chatting in front of the mosque when he felt the peculiar man's presence. The shaykh not only grasped his miraculous nature, but also caught a glimpse of his enigma, which had so confounded others. He resolved on the spot to seize hold of him, and to broadcast what he knew of his riddle to the crowd gathered around. But then his strength betrayed him completely—he could not move, nor could he speak.

Dream 60

I rang the bell and the door opened upon three young women whom I was sure I did not know, yet felt I was not seeing for the first time. I asked about the woman who owned the flat, and they replied that she was still on pilgrimage. No one knew when to expect her.

They walked me through the rooms of the apartment. Each time a door opened it would reveal a group of people around a circular dinner table immersed in pointed conversation—but due to the cacophony of their blended voices I couldn't make out anything they were discussing. I did not wish to enter any of the rooms, preferring to wait for the owner.

One of the young women informed me that the lady would be delayed by several days. In despair I replied that—after having taken part in futile discussions—I would rather defer all until the lady's return.

Dream 61

An invitation came to me to visit the house of a dear relative. Drawing near to his home, I saw crowds of invitees going inside. I realized that the invitation was a general one. Among those coming I saw a select group from the generation of our professors and another from that of my colleagues.

We exchanged greetings, then their conversation focused on the fact that all of them were living in Christopher Village. Many of them spoke about its beauty and its superiority over all the other touristic villages. We then entered, going to different tables to dine. My seat was at a tiny table stripped of all things, having not a tablecloth or plates or eating utensils or even food.

Before I could overcome my surprise I saw Shukuku coming toward me, grasping a leg of roasted mutton. He stuck it in my hand and went away laughing. Thunderstruck and annoyed, I saw no choice but to tear the meat with my fingers and to eat my food—although the whole time, all I could think of was Christopher Village.

Dream 62

A t last I found the ancient photograph among my old things. My joy was stillborn, however, when it quickly became clear that the picture had worn with the passage of time. My dear ones' features had been blotted so badly, there was nothing left of them but memories.

As fate would have it, I found myself in the waiting room of a government department, in my hand the service file of an employee who had been following in my footsteps, and who demanded a promotion. From experience I knew that the subject fell within the purview of the personnel department.

I looked for this office, but found no trace of it anywhere. As I passed before the storerooms, the door opened and out of it came a colleague whom God had taken from us a good month before. He seized the file from my hand and returned to the magazines, claiming that the subject was really his specialty.

His apparition made me forget what I had come there to do.

Dream 63

This green land was surrounded by a wall of medium height, enough to conceal what was happening within from those outside. From behind the wall projected an obelisk with a flag on its pinnacle, while the ground around it was covered with young people and their commotion.

At first I imagined this was an athletic club. But after looking about more carefully I became convinced it was a circus—for here was a group marching four abreast, and there was a troupe whose members traded shouts and kicks, while another group exchanged insults with every move. As for the rest of the youths, they sang anthems such as had never before been heard.

Wanting to learn more, I found myself beyond the great wall of the city, which a gigantic street sliced through. On both sides of the road, the crowds gathered outside the wall, their cheers rising up to the flag on top of the obelisk. Finally, the great door opened, from which issued a procession, car after car. In each car a young man sat in regal attitude, looking down at the people from on high, returning their greetings with contemptuous scorn.

Dream 64

I n horrific terror, my feet were nailed to the ground—for at only an arm's length from me, three huge, savage dogs were rearing up on their hind legs, ready to leap and tear me to pieces—if a woman hadn't daringly grabbed their tails.

On my right stood a female dog in the full splendor of youth, with a wondrously smooth, white coat, watching what was going on with an anxiety that showed in the constant twitchings of her short-cropped tail.

The three dogs' barking rose higher in a thunderous crescendo, the burning lust to destroy me gleaming in their eyes. Unable to get at me, they turned suddenly and pounced on the woman—and my heart was gripped by panic. Then the dogs threw themselves at me. As for the beautiful bitch, she stared at me for a while—then hesitated a fleeting moment before heedlessly plunging into the fray.

Dream 65

The academic year was done, and the date for the examination was declared. We hadn't once cracked a book nor memorized a sentence—and now we had to think about what to do.

A few of us still retained some respect for rationality, and so decided not to sit for the exam. The rest, however—afire with derision and mockery—seized the chance to show off by choosing to take the test anyway. On the famous morning we formed ourselves into lines and donned masks of seriousness and concern. Then the head of the committee stood up, announcing in a booming voice that he would hand out two papers to us. One of them contained the questions and the other the correct answers.

With this, we practically lost our minds—for we had not dreamed that any of our professors could possibly surpass us in the love of absurdity and the bizarre.

Dream 66

The owner and I came to an agreement—and the man invited me to inspect what we had reached agreement about. He showed me his beautiful apartment, his stunning wife, and her three-year old son. I was pleased with what I saw and so made an appointment for nine o'clock the next morning when the property would become mine.

An irresistible force drove me to the flat. The door opened— and it was the owner himself. Seeing me, he became enraged and slammed the door in my face, rattling the walls. I spent the night without sleeping, wondering with great agitation about Destiny and the slamming of the door.

Dream 67

A huge building—you wouldn't miss it. Originally it housed the ministry that employed me. When I saw young people going back to it, I too wanted to visit it. Inside I ran into a group of old colleagues and I was glad to see them. We walked from room to room and through memory after memory until we had made the past rise from its musty tomb. We passed a huge, amazing staircase and I immediately ascended to the third floor. There I found many young men. Whenever one of them would notice me, his face would frown at me disapprovingly.

My heart pounded. I felt the need to urinate. I looked here and there until my eyes settled upon an opening that led to a W.C. in a passage between the rooms. I scurried toward it to find workmen laboring diligently on the site—the project was not yet finished.

Going back whence I came, I quickly discovered there was no escape but by way of the street.

Dream 68

Such a gorgeous place. The sky and the ground and all between them were the color of white roses. The people were miracles of grace and serenity.

But its true miracle was that all the friends I've had in my life were gathered there, not only the living, but also the dead—though no one seemed the least bit surprised about those. We did not ask them what they had found in the other world, nor did they query us about what has happened on earth since their demise.

We all enjoyed this state so much, we wished it could go on and on. But it did not last—for black clouds descended from the heavens until darkness spread everywhere, separating us from each other. Rain poured down in waterfalls, followed by thunder and lightning, without any respite—until our hearts were in our throats.

Then some of our friends' voices began to penetrate our ears. One called out, "This is the end!"

A second shouted, "I see the gleam of an exit on the horizon!"

A third declared, "No matter what, there's no escaping the final reckoning."

Dream 69

In the center of this forest rose a hill in the shape of a pyramid. One climbed it through terraced stone passageways decorated with rows of date palms, beds of flowers, and shelters for lovers. I secluded myself with my sweetheart in one of these hideaways.

We swam together in a secret dialogue which removed all awareness of existence from our minds. Suddenly my companion stood up—and in the blink of an eye abandoned our refuge. I got up to catch her and to make sure that she was all right, when a voice like thunder came at me. Projected by an amplifier, it warned people of the presence of a time bomb, urging them to leave the hill immediately and without delay. Everyone rushed toward the rocky passageways. As I glanced around, a group of security forces joined us at a safe distance away.

I looked for my lover, but could find no trace of her anywhere: where could she have gone? Was there, then, any relationship between her and this crime? Would that not subject me, as well, to such an accusation, despite my innocence?

I heard the closest one of those who had stopped me say to his girlfriend that his heart told him, "The whole thing is false." I wondered if God believed the man's intuition, while I lingered—torn between thinking about my lost companion, and the expected explosion!

Dream 70

The longing to see my dear ones called to me, and I set off in the direction of the ancient quarter. As usual, I took a short cut on foot until the old house appeared, along with my memories.

I wasted no time in starting to climb toward the third and final floor. But halfway up the stairs, I was stricken by an exhaustion that would not pass, and which made me think about putting off the journey. If it weren't for my stubborn character—which hates to go back on a commitment—as well as for the intensity of my effort, I would not have made it until I reached the third-floor landing.

From my new vantage point, I could see the apartment door immersed in quiet and calm, and I realized that there were only ten more steps before the end of the staircase. Yet I did not see a single stair, finding in their place a deep pit. My heart pounded with fear for the people of the house.

Though it was now impossible to reach my goal, I did not look behind me. I did not think of going back, nor did I lose hope. I kept my eyes fixed on the door drowning in silence and tranquility—as I cried out, and cried out, and cried out again from somewhere deep within me.

Dream 71

He was the best in our young days, a truly rare kind of friend. Wondrously light of spirit, bright of repartee, elegant of reposte, brilliant at trading jibes, with a rich fund of stories, he was unusually gifted in all these fields. And he was always ready to join us whenever the occasion called for singing, dancing, or any form of amusement.

This is how we enjoyed our time together until he was chosen for a prestigious position known in our country for its gravitas and majesty. We watched apprehensively and soon our fears were realized, for he told us, as though replying to our anxiety, that he had decided to change his life from A to Z. No one questioned him on this as he bid us goodbye, commending us to God.

He would encounter us on public occasions, greeting us with an intense formality that deepened our feelings of estrangement and despair. Our old intimacy waned and practically disappeared, and we no longer heard of him except in the announcements of transfers and promotions. He began to fade from our consciousness until we nearly forgot him altogether. Time furthered our separation, until Fate decreed that we should meet by chance as our country was fêting its new national day—and we all came out to take part in the fun.

The drums were beaten as the brass band played. The army's troupe led the way, followed by that of the police, then the cars carrying the elite. Right ahead of them was our old friend, but in a state we would never have imagined—for we beheld him riding an ass. The clash between the inanity of his mount and the grandiosity of his dress was screamingly clear: the people laughed when he appeared.

Yet, it may truly be said, he looked neither to right or left, nor did he surrender a hair of his dignity.

Dream 72

The old house in Abbasiya was filled with the migratory birds—my brothers and sisters—on the day we had agreed to visit our mother. They asked me to have a meal of seafood prepared from the famous fish restaurant nearby.

Immediately I went to the restaurant and placed the order, and found that all of the tables were full except for the one nearest the door. I went over to it, sat down at one end of it and waited. Then a woman of about sixty, accompanied by a younger woman of around twenty, approached and sat down at the table. The waiter came with plates of *tagin*.

Unexpectedly, the older woman invited me to share their repast. Just as unexpectedly, I silently accepted the invitation and began to eat their food. No sooner had the waiter brought the meal wrapped up for the people at our house than I grabbed it, got up, and left without thanks or excuse. As I exited the restaurant I saw at but an arm's length away my departed friend, A. Sh., and was enormously pleased. Out of excessive courtesy I offered him the package. Without uttering a word he took it eagerly, before stepping through an open door—which he closed and locked behind him.

Astonished at his behavior, I had no choice but to return to the restaurant and make the order again. As the waiter brought sweets to the lady and her young companion, they invited me to share this with them; I did so without hesitation.

The woman told me that she wished to go to Shari' Bayn al-Sarayat, but did not know how to get there. I consented to take her and the three of us walked through the streets of Abbasiya. We became acquainted through the exchange of thanks and various kinds of conversation until we passed Shari' Bayn al-Sarayat without my noticing it.

I also forgot the food that was readied for me at the restaurant— just as I forgot the men and women waiting for me at the old house in Abbasiya.

Dream 73

Back in the old house in Abbasiya, I'm evidently annoyed because nothing came of my criticism, such as painting the walls or fixing the woodwork, the floors, and the furniture.

Then, from the far end of the flat, my mother's voice calls out in a sweet, pleasant tone that it's time I went out looking for a new apartment that would please me.

At this, the time and the place switch as I find myself in a reception hall, with many rooms and people. The way it looks reminds me of a government agency. This is confirmed by the arrival of my departed colleague, Mr. H.A., who informs me that the minister had sent a request to see me. Immediately I dashed to the minister's office, and, excusing myself, entered it—to find the man in other than his usual smiling state. He said that he had dreamed about my criticism of the revolution and its leader, which had wounded him grievously. I told him that I considered myself blindly infatuated with the principles of the revolution rather than being among those who opposed it—though I also always wished for its perfect completion, and for the avoidance of stumbles and setbacks.

Again I was taken through other times and places until I was a little boy meandering through Bayt al-Qadi Square. A friend my own age invited me to the wedding of his older brother. He said that his brother had invited Sa'd Zaghlul to officiate at the party and to give it his blessings—and that the great man had accepted, promising to attend. Utterly astounded, I told him, "Even more important than currently being prime minister, Sa'd Zaghlul is our nation's leader. What's more, you aren't among his relatives, or his comrades in the struggle."

"Sa'd truly is the nation's leader," the boy rejoined, "and singles out the simple people for his affection"—adding that I would see for myself.

At the appointed time I went to the feast in Crimson Lane, where my friend guided me into a room. There—in the place of honor—I saw Sa'd Zaghlul, wearing the suit of the master of ceremonies, sitting down with him. The two were engrossed in conversation, laughing hard together. I was so dazzled by what I saw that it rooted itself in my depths forever.

Dream 74

The giant playing field sat in the place of the neighbors' houses on the opposite side of the street, filled with British soldiers singing and dancing about. Disturbed and uneasy, we followed them, then they scattered down our street and those branching off from it.

We thought the matter over, fixing our attention on the move from one part of town to another. Not finding a proper house we contented ourselves with a stately apartment, sparing no effort until it was worthy to live in. We had just about settled comfortably into the place when we heard a rustling sound of the sort usually made by mice. Our leisure was spoiled. But before we could think of what to do, we heard someone banging on the outside door.

Opening the door, I saw many men armed with sticks. They said they were residents of the building who were chasing a thief—who, they thought, had fled into our flat. Forcing their way into our apartment, they ransacked the rooms, making a dreadful racket—only to announce that they had not found the fugitive.

After having turned our home upside down, they left without having caught the vanished crook. As we exchanged looks of irritation and rage, we once again heard the same rustling sound. Furious, I declared that—whether a mouse, a thief, or a demon— I would not open the door for anyone banging again.

Dream 75

My mother greeted our dear neighbor and her beautiful daughter in the living room on the third floor of our old house. I was invited to sit with them out of trust in the friendship between our two families. During all the chatter I stared at the daughter and she stared at me—this was not lost on her mother. As she left the room, the neighbor woman whispered to me, "You two should go down together to the floor below as is customary among members of the family." I accepted the invitation with perplexity and perfect joy. No sooner had we entered the floor below when I drew her close—but before I could go the next step I heard a strange commotion as the place was overrun with women and men and teenagers, splitting off into different rooms.

Then a man from State Security came and stood before the door, declaring that he would uphold the law, and I nearly went crazy with confusion. My bewilderment doubled when I saw the others singing in one room, and dancing in another. I looked to my girlfriend pleading for salvation, only to find her calm and smiling.

At that, I decided to flee—but found the security man at the exit. I was stuck there motionless, a prey to befuddlement, and dashed by despair.

Dream 76

Beneath this leafy tree sat my friend from my early days who was martyred for love of country. Though it had been decades since his death, he looked quite elegant and in the pink of health and cheer.

The sight of him made my chest flutter as I rushed toward him—but he halted me with a wave of his walking stick. I reminded him of our time as friends, but he paid no heed to my words—saying that he had run out of patience regarding the neighborhood rubbish heap.

After this speech, he threw down his stick and went away, leaving me sad. Yet I swelled up with a new spirit and hurried immediately to the trash pile, raining a hail of blows all over it with his cane. Each blow cut a gap in it: from each gap men and women emerged whose general appearance was unlike garbage.

Indeed, they were models of cleanliness, prestige, and respectability. Each time one of them appeared, they jumped with terror of the rod in my hand. Following this, I became utterly convinced that the sun would rise tomorrow over a world of greenery and pristine air.

Dream 77

I turned onto the quiet side street carrying my overnight bag. Instantly I met memories and passions, encircled by peril and trepidation.

I expected to be scolded for my long absence; hence I'd prepared the appropriate excuses.

Reaching the building's entrance, I saw the flat on the ground floor, four steps away from the staircase. Grinning broadly, I pressed the buzzer eagerly. The peep window opened to reveal a strange man dressed in a house robe who seemed to be the place's owner. Suddenly my burning passion plunged to the bottom of a freezing lake. Quickly I concocted a phoney story to extricate myself from this impasse. I said I was looking for the residence of the schoolteacher, So-and-So Effendi, but had come to the wrong building.

Searching my face with wary suspicion, the man said, "This is his flat—he's inside. What's your name, sir, so that I may tell him you're here?"

I realized that I had been found out and had lost face. Raising his voice, the man shouted, "You're nothing but a vicious liar, like all who've come here before you!"

Not able to bear more, I scurried away in defeat, nearly losing my balance. The bag dropped from my hand, exposing a bottle of wine and a kilogram of kabab on a paper plate. But I could think of one thing only: to vanish with lightning speed.

Dream 78

Such a gigantic funeral—I didn't know how to join the procession. I didn't know anyone walking in it, not even the man who had died. The strangest thing is that the funeral took a route not used before, heading off toward a network of railroad tracks. We crossed over them into the wasteland, than paused for rest.

During this time, the trains heading north and south arrived. This sparked an argument among those gathered around the bier. One group wanted to carry it to the south, and the other to the north. Both claimed that they were carrying out the wish of the deceased. One of the wise men called out to remind them that the dearly departed was among the righteous friends of God—and would never permit anyone to carry him in an unsatisfactory direction.

We all contemplated the sanctity of what he said. The southern-bound troupe tried to carry the bier, but was unable, while the northerners also hazarded their luck, only to meet with failure, too. At that point everyone realized that the saint didn't want to leave the place where he was, lying between south and north.

Dream 79

I sat on the balcony of the little hotel overlooking the sea, so absorbed in waiting for my girlfriend that I was oblivious to the gorgeous view. As the waiting dragged on, the hotel manager, who happened to be a childhood friend, came over to suggest that I cure myself of my worry by taking a walk.

I went to the shore where I kept marching back and forth, until I spotted my lover in a swimming race with a group of young men. One of them went with her out of sight behind a rock. I felt a stabbing pain in my heart and an unfathomable frustration. Sensing this, the manager said, "That's the way of the world—don't surrender to sadness."

"You know, I know many things," I replied, "but I don't know how to swim." So he took me to a quiet corner of the hotel garden, where I spent a distressed and anxious hour. Then, to my complete surprise, my girlfriend came toward me, her face grinning with happiness. I leapt up to pour out the weight of my anger, and in so doing encountered yet another surprise—completely unexpected, and incomprehensible, too, defying any explanation. For I was suddenly overcome with limitless joy as the grief was wiped out of my breast altogether, as if it had never been there. And so we greeted each other, in the way we always had in the past.

We walked around the city, as we usually did. Passing a gift shop, we went inside without wavering, heading straight for the department devoted to engagements and weddings.

My lover's eyes studied the innumerable items. Finally she said, "We don't have enough time."

"We have all time," I innocently replied.

Dream 80

We gathered in the old room: my mother, my four sisters, and me. No sooner had we closed the door upon ourselves than complaints arose about times past and people we knew.

My mother turned toward me apprehensively, swearing an oath that all she had ever done or said was out of the purest love. At this, voices were raised, demanding, "If that's true, then how do you explain what happened?"

Scoldingly, my mother replied, "You have to account for yourselves, as well: don't try to tell me it was all written and decreed."

Dream 81

At long last I went to the mansion. I asked the doorman to inform the eminent woman that the winner of her literary prize had come to present his thanks in person, if only she would permit him.

The man soon returned to bring me into the reception hall, whose beauty and vastness dazzled me. Before long a musical tune signaling welcome was played for me—and I spied the enchanting figure of the madam moving gracefully to its rhythm. I undertook to present my letter of thanks—but she, with a chic sweep of her hands, opened up her breasts, drawing from between them a neat little gun.

She pointed it at me. I forgot the letter—fainting away before she could pull the tiny pistol's trigger.

Dream 82

I was pleased that the new director had taken over the institute's affairs—though I had not taken part in his selection. Yet every time I spoke appreciatively of him, my colleagues attacked me with sarcasm. This left me confused between approval on one side, and derision on the other. But I refused absolutely ever to despair.

Dream 83

I watched the cart carrying the enchantress of Crimson Lane coming, and drawing it was a winged stallion. I got in and sat at the rear. The steed responded by spreading its wings, and the cart began to fly until we were higher than the rooftops and minarets—and in seconds we arrived at the Great Pyramid's pinnacle. We started to pass over it from an arm's height above it. But then I rashly leapt down onto the pyramid's summit, my eyes never parting from the seductive girl as she soared upward and upward—and the nightfall descended, the darkness ever deepening, until she was fixed in the heavens as a luminous star.

Dream 84

I dreamed I was on the Street of Love, as I used to call it in my hopeful youth. I dreamed that I sauntered between grand houses and gardens perfumed with flowers. But where was the mansion of my worshipped one? Gone without a trace, its place had been taken by a huge mosque of majestic dimensions, of magnificent design, with the tallest and most graceful of minarets. I was shocked. As I stood there in a stupor, the muezzin started the call for the sunset prayer. Without tarrying I went into the mosque, praying with the worshippers. When the prayers were finished, I moved slowly, as though not wanting to leave. Hence I was the last one departing to reach the door. There I discovered that my shoes had gone missing—and I had to find my own way out.

Dream 85

A tram station—and I was confused as to where in it I should wait for mine to arrive. But I was really awaiting the radiant face of the beauty in the window overlooking the stop, at which I kept on staring and staring.

My longing went on and on, and how many of my friends had asked me how long my torture would continue? Yet I was going on a trip that I could not avoid, as though it were Fate or Destiny. In truth, it was a strenuous, debilitating journey, much longer that I thought it would be. And on my return, the only thing that I could make out was a square-shaped enclosure, which was the window.

I spotted her within it, but she appeared to be mute, neither asking questions, nor answering them. As in the past, I stood beneath the aperture indifferent to the passers-by, until finally the sound of a conversation drifted down, like a whisper mingled with discreet laughter.

I heard a voice wonder, "What's this guy's story, the one who's hanging around under the window?"

"He's blubbering over the memory of a sweetheart—and her house," came her giggling reply.

Dream 86

I was entrusted with carrying a letter to the late Dr. Husayn Fawzi. I told him that I had brought with me a proposal to restore him to the service with a significant increase in salary. He would also receive a luxurious office.

The doctor laughed, saying that the pay didn't interest him, nor did the office. What mattered was respect for his ideas and his dignity.

I backed away, secure in the knowledge that my mission had failed.

Dream 87

The crime was discovered early in the morning. Before long, the story of its beastliness was on every tongue. Yet I couldn't find anywhere to hide because the whole place was crisscrossed with policemen and female psychiatrists. I was in total panic until the greatest of the lady shrinks invited me to her office.

She told me that the majority of her colleagues attributed the crime's brutality to the latent cruelty in the perpetrator's character. She, however, thought it was due to the killer's inexperience, as well as his ignorance of the modern scientific bases for the art of murder. For this reason she had decided to enroll him in the Institute for Contemporary Criminality—and may God grant him success!

Dream 88

In our village, every individual was waiting for the letter that would settle their personal destiny. One day, I received my own letter—and read it to find I had been condemned to death by hanging.

Word spread far and wide, as was customary among us. The members of our village club met and decided to celebrate the event when it happened.

In my house, where I lived with my mother, brothers, and sisters, breasts were gladdened and all were pleased. On the much-anticipated day, the drums pounded in the club. I came out of my house wearing my finest clothes, surrounded by the members of my family.

But then my mother, separating herself from our state of mind, began to cry. If only my father had lived long enough, she wailed, to see for himself this glorious day.

Dream 89

From my position in the garden I could see a lady of sixty coming toward me, her face frowning. Angrily, she snarled, "Because of you, I lost the prize."

I recalled the woman and her upset face—but I couldn't get the meaning of what she was saying. She kept repeating, "The committee disqualified my story on the pretext that it was a copy of your story published forty years ago."

Suddenly everything became clear. I could see that bad luck still plagued her as she told me, "I swore to them my story could not be so accused, simply because it's my own biography."

Exasperated, I replied, "I certainly agree: I lifted bits from the events of your life in which I played a despicable role."

The woman answered, laughing sarcastically, "Here's a chance for me to be your victim in real life—and not just in fiction."

Dream 90

The building of the house was finished: an architectural marvel, people from all over gathered around it, each hoping to possess it. The haggling increased and the arguments intensified until a giant cut through the crowd, roaring in a ringing voice, "Force is the answer."

The people fell silent—except for one man, who answered the challenge. A feverish battle raged between them until the giant was able to deal a blow to his opponent's head, knocking him unconscious. Then the giant broke into the house and locked it up completely after him.

The hours passed without the door opening to provide a chance for vengeance. Those standing outside took no useful action, while seeming as though they would not disperse.

Dream 91

In the beginning was the wagon. I was pushing it before me with power and mirth. One day I found a little girl atop it, and became even more active and gay. Then more people kept coming until they covered the whole wagon, sapping away all my strength and merriment. The riders sensed my sufferings. I determined to abandon the wagon as soon as a good opportunity arose. With the passage of days, the wagon emptied, returning to the way it was before. As for me, I didn't go back, but grew weaker and weaker, until finally I became indifferent to the wagon, and collapsed beside it.

Dream 92

There I was in a radiant reception hall. In my hands was a golden platter filled with all manner of delectable delights.

I was reminded of the brilliant evening companions among our lifelong friends who had left this world. I began to see them approaching, their resonant laughter preceding them. We traded salaams of greeting, as they began to praise the platter and what it presented. Yet my happiness was suddenly extinguished when I exclaimed that I could not partake with them, for the doctors had categorically forbidden me ever to smoke.

Surprise showed on their faces as they scrutinized me intensely. They asked dismissively, "Are you still afraid of Death?"

Dream 93

On top of a nearby home I spied furniture, wrapped and decorated. Then I remembered that I'd heard the house's owner had turned the place into a cultural institute for which he charged no admission: he was content to live on the roof.

Pleased by this, I admired him for it, and was invited to attend some of his lessons. I found the place crammed with humanity. The man said today's lesson would be about the bull that bore the world on his horn. His speech struck me as odd, and a derisory laugh escaped me. Faces glazed with anger turned toward me.

The man himself fixed me with a glowering stare, silently pointing to the door.

Dream 94

Five men wielding switchblades seized me: I gave them my money and they fled with confusing speed. Yet some of their features remained imprinted in my memory. Since that incident, I have avoided walking alone on the side streets, though the main road is never devoid of its own ordeals. One day I found the traffic stopped and the people gathered on either side.

Before long came a convoy of many cars. As the last part of it passed before me, I saw a face that made my heart leap, and began to mutter, "There must be so many who look the same."

Dream 95

The journey's start was agreed. The family met the news contentedly, hastening to advance me money. I went immediately to the tailor to be fitted for a suit in the latest fashion, and the man truly did an outstanding job. Still, he wasn't satisfied.

Producing an elegant turban, he thrust it on my head. "Now," he said, "the suit's in the current style."

Dream 96

The fighting grew fiercer along the roads until its rattle and ruckus brought all means of transport to a complete halt. I returned exhausted to my home—where I longed to lighten my tiredness under the water of my shower. When I went into the bath, I found my girl inside, drying off her nude body. Completely transformed, I rushed toward her, but she pushed me far away from her—warning that the warring in the streets was growing closer to my house.

Dream 97

ere was the office of the Secretariat, where I spent a lifetime before going on pension. Here, too, I had been companion to the cream of employees, in all of whose funerals Fate decreed that I take part.

I stared inside the room to see the youths who had succeeded us, and was nearly felled by the shock—for I found no one there but my old colleagues. I rushed inside, shouting, "God's peace upon my dear ones!" with anticipation, confusion, and unease. Yet not one of them raised his head from his papers, and I withdrew back unto myself in frustration and despair.

When the time came to go, they left their places without any of them turning to look at me—not even the lovely lady translator. And so I found myself alone in the empty chamber.

Dream 98

From my prospect on the sidewalk, I cast my gaze onto the garden enclosed by the iron fence. There I saw the queen of my heart as she dispensed chocolates to lovers gathered there.

I raced toward the fence's gate until I reached the entrance, panting as I ran inside. But I found not a trace of my dear one, and cried out a curse upon love. The time came for me to go back outside—and there I saw my girlfriend in the same place where I had been, walking arm-in-arm with a young man who appeared to be her fiancé.

I wanted to return whence I came, but exhaustion, prolonged reflection, and the lost opportunity would not let me.

Dream 99

This was a circular field in whose center was a slender date palm, and around which little houses were clustered. In the afternoon, the doors would open and women would come out to chat under the palm. Usually the conversation was about marriage and their daughters. I would withdraw far away to follow what they were saying with zeal.

When the sun set I would be devoured by hunger. No one would know of my condition except for my childhood girlfriend who would slink up to me carrying a small plate, one half of it filled with white cheese, the other smothered in parsley.

We would labor together to assuage each other's hunger, to the hum of the gossip about who would be wedding whom.

Dream 100

This is a trial and this a bench and sitting at it is a single judge and this is the seat of the accused and sitting at it is a group of national leaders and this is the courtroom, where I have sat down longing to get to know the party responsible for what has befallen us. But I grow confused when the dialogue between the judge and the leaders is conducted in a language I have never before heard, until the magistrate adjusts himself in his seat as he prepares to announce the verdict in the Arabic tongue. I lean forward to hear, but then the judge points at me—to pronounce a sentence of death upon me. I cry out in alarm that I'm not part of this proceeding and that I'd come of my own free will simply to watch and see—but no one even notices my scream.

Dream 101

We prettied up the house to welcome back the son—during his time away, he'd become a celebrity. We spent the evening on our balcony with its beautiful view and its cleansing breeze, as the prodigal one entertained us with poetry and songs well into the night.

But in the morning we found the balcony's entrance blocked by a monstrous wardrobe. I felt ashamed—nor did our son hide his dismay when it dawned on him that folks from the heart of his family detested his presence, despising his delightful work.

Dream 102

A t length I went down to the toilet on the lower floor of the old house. Soon, however, I became annoyed with its dampness and discomfort, and went out searching all over again until I wound up on the upper floor. This was better than all the other areas, but then it rained with unusual intensity. The water ran down from the roof and forced us to heap up the furniture and to cover it completely, following which we fled the flat for the stairwell. When it dawned on the new resident of the lower level that we were there, he came out to us—inviting us with extreme insistence to go inside where it was warm, safe, and dry.

Dream 103

What's happening in our house? All the chairs are lined up with their feet nailed down and the ceilings are stripped of their lamps and the walls of their pictures and the floors of their carpets—so what's going on in our house?

They say it's all to protect our home against the many burglaries of apartments. But I reply without pause that a break-in would be dearer to my heart than ugliness and chaos.

Dream 104

I saw myself in Abbasiya wandering in the vastness of my memories, recalling in particular the late Lady Eye. So I contacted her by telephone, inviting her to meet me by the fountain, and there I welcomed her with a passionate heart.

I suggested that we spend the evening together in Fishawi Café, as in our happiest days. But when we reached the familiar place, the deceased blind bookseller came over to us and greeted us warmly—though he scolded the dearly departed Eye for her long absence.

She told him what had kept her away was Death. But he rejected that excuse—for Death, he said, can never come between lovers.

Glossary

Azbakiya: The name of both a large park in central Cairo and the district surrounding it. Established ca. 1476 by a local dignitary, the Amir Azbak—after whom it is named—around a small lake, for nearly five centuries it remained one of the wealthiest and most desired quarters in Cairo. The lake disappeared in the early nineteenth century, and most of the area's grandeur by the latter part of the twentieth.

Bayt al-Qadi Square: Naguib Mahfouz was born into a middle-class household at 8 Bayt al-Qadi Square (Judge's House Square) at the corner of Darb Qirmiz (Crimson Lane) in the old Islamic quarter of Cairo on December 10, 1911. (The birth was not registered until the following day; hence he observes his birthday on December 11 each year.) The "judge's house," built some time before 1800, stands at the southwest edge of the square next to the ruins of the ornately decorated palace of the fifteenth-century amir Mamay. The name refers to its service as a courthouse during the last century of Ottoman rule in Egypt (1517–1914).

birth-feast of Husayn: Part of the popular Egyptian tradition of fêting the birthdays of holy persons, the largest one is that for the Prophet Muhammad's grandson, Husayn (Hussein). Many thousands gather around the Husayn Mosque (where it is claimed the saint's head is kept) in al-Gamaliya for the occasion. The date of the celebration varies each year in accordance with the lunar-based Islamic calendar.

Christopher Village: Apparently an invention of Mahfouz's mind, perhaps inspired by St. Christopher's Village, a budget tourist hotel in London. Mahfouz had successful surgery in that city to remove an aneurism in his abdominal aorta in 1991, the first and only time he has been to the United Kingdom.

fuul: Broad beans—also known as horse beans—an indispensable part of the Egyptian diet, including the author's own.

gallabiya*:* A long, loose garment commonly worn by Egyptians.

Ghuriya: Part of the main north–south thoroughfare in the Islamic district of Cairo, named for the surviving façades of a mosque and mausoleum built in 1504–05 by the Sultan Qansuh al-Ghuri, who died in 1516 vainly resisting the Ottoman conquest of Egypt and the Levant, which inexorably followed in 1517.

al-Hagg Ali: "Pilgrim Ali," a person known to Mahfouz in his native district of al-Gamaliya, who at least into the mid-1990s apparently owned much property in Bayt al-Qadi Square (see above).

Harafish*:* in this instance, a group of friends—mostly actors, artists, writers, and musicians—to which Naguib Mahfouz has belonged since roughly 1942, and which until recently met every Thursday evening without fail. The word itself is the plural of *harfush*, which originally may have been defined as "a person without a skilled trade." By the nineteenth century, it generally meant "poor person," or even "riff-raff." One of the Mahfouz group's most prominent members, the late actor Ahmed Mazhar (1917–2002)— who is thought to have given the weekly association its name— said that a *harfush* is "the *agent provocateur* found at the edge of every demonstration."

Husayn district: Named for the Mosque of al-Husayn, which it surrounds, this is part of the larger district of Gamaliya, itself the northern (and largest) section of the former royal city of the Shiite Fatimid dynasty (969–1171). Known as al-Qahira, the Fatimids' exclusive seat of power eventually formed the core of what became modern Cairo.

kunafa*:* Vermicelli baked in sugar, honey, and melted butter.

jellaba*:* A North African garment similar to the Egyptian gallabiya (see above), though usually featuring a hood.

jubba*:* A wide-sleeved, long outer garment, open in front.

mahmal*:* Until the advent of easy motorized travel, it was customary for Egyptian and other Islamic rulers to send a camel-borne litter, or mahmal, to Mecca bearing an elaborately embroidered cloth to decorate the Kaaba, or sacred cube-shaped black stone in the holy sanctuary, during the annual Muslim pilgrimage.

rabab: A primitive, usually one-to-three-stringed instrument frequently used to accompany the recital of heroic folk epics, ballads, and other songs.

Rose of the Nile: A name given to differing varieties of aquatic plants that grow in the Nile through the length of Egypt.

Shari' Bayn al-Sarayat: "Between the Palaces Street," a thoroughfare next to Cairo University (formerly the Egyptian University, from which Mahfouz graduated with a B.A. in Philosophy in 1934) in the western Cairo suburb of al-Giza. Not to be confused with Shari' Bayn al-Qasrayn in Gamaliya, literally "Between the Two Palaces," but rendered *Palace Walk* as the title of the English translation of *Bayn al-qasrayn*, the first volume of Mahfouz's *Cairo Trilogy*.

shaykh of the *hara*: A resident put in charge by the authorities to watch over the affairs of a neighborhood (*hara*, which also means alley or side street) in traditional parts of Cairo.

Shaykh Zakariya Ahmad: Celebrated singer, *'ud* player (see below), and composer (1896–1961), and a close friend of Naguib Mahfouz. Trained at Egypt's principal Islamic school, al-Azhar, he authored a number of highly popular works sung by Egypt's greatest diva, Umm Kulthoum (1904?–75), and also created numerous operettas.

Shukuku: Mahmud Shukuku (1912–85) was a popular Egyptian comedian, actor, and singer of monologs. He appeared in over one hundred films between 1944 and 1976.

Sidi Gaber: The first train stop in Alexandria. Mahfouz has compared his current, advanced stage of life to that of a person pulling into Sidi Gaber Station, knowing that the final destination is a but a short time away. (See *Naguib Mahfouz at Sidi Gaber: Reflections of a Nobel Laureate 1994–2001*, from conversations with Mohamed Salmawy, AUC Press, 2001.)

tagin: A dish of meat and vegetables baked in individual pots in a rich tomato sauce.

'ud: A multi-stringed instrument, the Arab version of the lute.